Call Me Brick

Munroe Howard

Call Me Brick

Grove Press, Inc., New York

To Maggie

I guess it all started that summer, seven years ago, when my guardian insisted on shipping me off to camp, to learn how to get along with other girls my age, and get used to the idea that I couldn't just live in my own world surrounded by men all the time, and interested only in my own wishes and my own pleasures. Just how much I did learn, and the direction in which some of this learning went, was as much a surprise to him as it was to me. But before I get too far into these memoirs, maybe it would be a good idea to explain a little about myself, so my readers will understand what I am talking about.

I was born a few months over sixteen years ago, and christened Brittania MacLean by my parents. But nobody can go through life with a name like Brittania, so everyone just calls me Brick. I never did find out for certain whether my red hair had anything to do with my nickname, but it doesn't matter too much because my real name is so terrible, I never mention it to a soul. Whenever I went to a new school, I always got in dutch with the principal because I insisted my name was Brick. I never did get a chance to tell my parents what I thought of their choice as they were both killed in an automobile accident when I was **two,** leaving me an orphan without a blood relative in the world. After that, I went to live with my guardian, Jackson Brant, a bachelor who was my father's best friend. He's tall and dreamy looking, and his hair is curly in a way that sends shivers down a girl's back, even when she's beyond the age of being a girl and has become a woman. He stood in for my father and mother for fourteen years with a lot of success, but he never really knew what to make of me. Sometimes I think he was even a little afraid of me. Which only made us even because there were lots of times I was more than a little afraid of him. When those big gray eyes of his started to shine, it was more than I could bear and very scary. Sometimes I wished he'd smack my bottom for me and get it over with, but he was one of those dopes who didn't believe in hitting children. He thought it would leave deeper marks on my mind than it would on my bottom, which only shows how silly he could be. But most of the time he was out of this world, and I loved him like crazy. I even dreamed about him at night, and woke up wishing he'd fall in love with me and stop thinking of me as a little pest, whose nose had to be wiped for her as well as her other end, both of which jobs he took care of many times.

Anyway, up to that summer I was nine, we were together all the time. Even when he went on fishing trips with his friends he'd take me along, treating me more like a boy than a girl. When it got cold, we'd share the same sleeping bag. We'd go swimming together completely naked, and we'd even squat down behind the bushes together when it was necessary. Of course, being a man and all, he didn't have to do as much squatting as I did. In those days, I used to blame God for using up all of his better supplies when he made Adam. Because when he finally got to Eve, he didn't have enough stuff left to give her outside plumbing in front too. And this can be an awful pain when a girl is wearing blue jeans and long drawers in the woods and the weather's real nippy. But when I got to be nine, some of his friends, females of course, started saying it wasn't right for a girl to be with a man all the time. They insisted I should be sent to summer camp, to find out what it was like to be with other little girls. And being only a man, he didn't catch on. I knew they just didn't want me hanging around, watching everything they did. But like a fool, he thought they were only interested in my welfare, instead of their own. And where my welfare was concerned, everything else took second place with Jackson Brant.

But after that first summer at Camp Winnepesaukee, I stopped being just another little girl, and learned a few things about what it meant to be a female.

The inside of my tent was dark when I came in, seeming even darker because the sun was so bright outside. And was it hot! The other kids in my group were in the assembly hall, working on their costumes for the silly show they expected to put on for the visitors over the weekend. I got myself excused by playing sick. Jack had never taught me how to sew, and I wasn't anxious to learn. All I wanted to do was to go back to my tent, take off all my clothes, and just stretch out

9

on my cot. That's what we always did at home when the weather got too hot.

I didn't notice Betsy on her cot until I was lying naked on mine. Then I heard a tiny noise, looked around, and saw her for the first time. She was naked too. But instead of just lying there letting the sweat roll off, she seemed to be moving her bottom up and down, and it must have been the squeak that I had heard. She was flat on her back with both hands pressed into her vag, and she was breathing like she'd been running as hard as she could. I got scared, because she looked so strange, and went over to see what was wrong. That's one thing Jack always taught me. When anyone was in trouble, it was the duty of other people to try to help. But just as I reached the side of her cot, Bet sort of sighed, dropped her hands to her sides, and lay back with a dreamy look on her face.

"What's the matter? You sick?" I asked.

"No."

"What were you doing?"

"Enjoying myself, nosy," she giggled. "Why don't you do the same?"

"But your hands were in your vag. Why?"

"Stop calling it a vag!" snorted Bet. "It's my pussy!"

"Jack always called mine a vag," I insisted. "And I guess he ought to know more about me than you do, seeing he brought me up."

"Gosh you're stupid!" snickered Bet. "Every girl has a pussy."

"What are you talking about?"

"Ever see a big girl . . . naked?"

"I see them naked around here every day. Even counselors . . . sometimes."

"Well, with all that hair in front, doesn't it look like they've got a pussy shoved between their legs?"

"I guess maybe it does."

"Even men have hair . . . there."

"I know that, silly."

"Ever see a boy . . . naked?"

"No."

"They're cute . . . with no hair to get in the way. Just like us."

"I still want to know what you were doing when I came in."

"Coming."

"No. I was the one who was coming in."

Bet eyed me for a moment with a secret kind of look. Then she patted the top of the blanket next to her. "Sit down here while I explain a few things to you," she said. "You talk just like a baby."

I flopped down willingly. "Explain what?"

"Do you know what grown-ups do?"

"Of course!"

"Know what it's called?"

"Sure! Fucking!"

"Ever see anyone do it?"

"Yeah. I watched Jack a few times with one of his girl friends. But he doesn't know it—thank goodness!"

"Would he be mad?"

"Wouldn't your dad?"

"He'd kill me. Anyway, remember when I got sick last week and spent the night in the infirmary?"

"I sure do! You cried and didn't want to go. You were afraid the nurse'd give you an enema."

"She did. But she did something else first. She

11

showed me how I can do the same thing grown-ups do . . . all by myself."

"How?"

"She took me on her lap, kissed my pussy a few times, and then put her fingers inside it. She kept moving them about till suddenly the whole room exploded. I don't know what really happened, but I felt better than I ever did before. Miss Wilson told me that's what happens when grown-up people fuck. After a while, I did the same thing for her. We had lots of fun. Now I go back every night after everyone is asleep."

"You kissed her . . . pussy?"

"Yeah," Bet giggled. "The hair tickled something awful too."

"Will you show me . . . how to do it?"

"Miss Wilson will."

"How do you know?"

"Because she told me to be sure and bring any other girls who wanted to learn to her, so she could be sure they were taught properly. But she warned me not to talk about the fun we have to other counselors. You have to promise too."

"O.K. Let's go right now."

"No. Tonight . . . after everyone is asleep. I'll tell Miss Wilson at supper I'm bringing you with me."

Before I go any further, I guess maybe I ought to do a little explaining, so whoever reads this will have some idea of what kind of people I'm writing about, myself included. Just because a person is grown-up and crammed full of all kinds of education and experience doesn't mean he knows as much as he thinks he does about the world, or even those closest to him. I have found this out myself, now that I'm past sixteen and practically through growing. And my guardian is a perfect example of what I'm talking about. Jack always rated himself as a very liberal-minded person. At least he always boasted he was whenever he got into a discussion with any of his friends, which was only all the time. Naturally, he was a great believer in every one of the new ideas that have become popular during the last thirty years or so. And Progressive Education was almost number one on his list, along with a few other things like a feeling for modern art, a disbelief in a rigid code of morals for anyone, and a strong dislike for censorship of any kind. Everyone connected with Camp Winnepesaukee, of course, was also a believer, which is why Jack chose it for me in the first place. It's motto was: "Free Expression for Every Camper in Everything!" And when I say that went for everything, I mean everything. Piss, shit, fuck, pussy, and pecker were heard all day long in casual conversation in any group from eight to eighteen. Not that there were any peckers around for us to talk about. Unfortunately for our growing, thirsty minds, the camp wasn't coed. The only male organ on the grounds, except on visitors' days, belonged to Mr. Gunther, the direc-tress' husband. And I guess maybe Mrs. Gunther wasn't as much of a believer as she liked people to think, because whenever Mr. Gunther showed up on the weekends, she'd never let him get near any of the campers or the counselors, unless she was right there with him. My wonderful guardian, and the families of the other girls who went there, never had the vaguest notion of the trouble we got into, or the habits we picked up, because of the complete lack of supervision.

That night, when Bet and I tiptoed into the infirmary after the other girls in our tent were asleep, we found Miss Wilson drinking coffee and talking to Mary Ann, one of the better-liked counselors in camp. Mary Ann was a college student who taught tennis, and she was the kind of girl who always seemed to be laughing. Of course, her figure was wonderful from all that exercise, and she was always happy to show it off, naked or dressed, to anyone who was interested, even us kids. She was even ready to demonstrate to some of the older girls, who were disappointed at the size of their tits, the proper exercises to build themselves up. And believe me, hers were magnificent.

I was excited and a little scared because I didn't know what to expect, but Bet had been there enough times already to feel right at home. As soon as we got inside, she took off her robe and pajamas and hopped around naked. After giving each of us a mug of coffee, both Miss Wilson and Mary Ann smiled encouragingly at me. They could see I was nervous, and they tried very hard to make me feel at ease. Mary Ann, of course, knew why I was there, but she let Miss Wilson talk first.

"I'm glad you came, Brick."

"Thank you, ma'am."

"Bet told me you were anxious to learn how to play our little game."

"Bet says it's fun."

"Tell me, do you know anything about masturbation?"

14

"I don't even know what it means. I just watched Bet once."

"Did what she was doing and where she put her hands bother you at all?"

"No, ma'am."

"Do you like boys, Brick?" Mary Ann asked softly.

"They're O.K. . . . I guess."

Mary Ann got up and came over to stand in front of me. "Deep down inside, don't you think they're messy little creatures . . . dirty and smelly?"

"Sometimes."

"You don't sound very sure."

"The only boy I know well is my guardian . . . and he's a man."

"Has he ever talked to you about . . . pussy-petting?"

"No."

"Has he ever played with you himself?"

"Oh, yes, ma'am! We play tennis together all the time."

"I mean . . . does he ever play with your body?"

"Sure! He pats my bottom."

"Often?"

"Every chance he gets—but usually when I'm drying off after my shower in the mornings, or when I get undressed to go to bed at night."

"What do you do?"

"I giggle."

"Do you like to have your bottom patted?"

"Don't you?"

After a quick look at Miss Wilson, Mary Ann reached her hand and took mine, pulling me to my feet. "Brick," she said gently, "I think you and I should go into the other room for a while.

15

I'm sure Bet and Miss Wilson would rather be by themselves in here."

"O.K."

An hour or so later, when Bet and I stumbled back to our tent, I was exhausted, but I felt better and more grown-up than I would have thought possible for a girl of nine. And it wasn't at all strange when you consider what I'd been through. I'd had my bottom patted more than it had ever been before. I'd learned what it felt like to have my pussy kissed and what it felt like to kiss someone else's. I'd learned what it felt like to have it rubbed and to rub someone else's. And I'd learned what it felt like to have Mary Ann's finger stuck up my asshole and to do the same to hers. I'd learned about life, so I thought, and I'd liked everything I had learned.

Time is supposed to fly only when you're old, but it can pass by just as quickly when you're young. I know it, because it seemed like yesterday that Bet and I sneaked into the infirmary to learn the ins and outs of pussy-petting. Yet suddenly, it was four years later, with me at the ripe old age of thirteen. Lots had happened since that night, not only to everyone else but to me as well. But no matter where I end up in life, I will always remember good old Camp Winnepesaukee as the place where I got my start. Someday, I suppose, a high-priced psychiatrist will be able to trace everything I am, and everything I will be, to the lessons I learned, and the habits and tastes I developed, in the woods of New England at that summer camp for girls from good families.

Some months before, I'd finally become a com-

16

plete woman for the first time, and already I didn't like it at all. It turned out to be a terrible pain, and I could have done very well without it. One reason, I guess, was that I kept forgetting how necessary it was to pay attention to the calendar. Twice I'd had to run home with my clothes in a mess because I couldn't seem to remember. But my figure really had started to look more feminine. I was getting rounder in all the right places, and up on top I filled out the front of my dresses with me, instead of those rolled up hankies I used to stuff in there to look a little more like a girl. You might think this was a big joke, but it was pretty important to me. I still had an awfully long way to go before I could equal someone like Mary Ann, but I did her special exercises everyday, and even Jack was beginning to notice the improvement. He never said anything to me, of course, but I could see it in his eyes whenever he happened to see me naked, which I made sure to let him do at least several times a week. For some reason, he didn't pat my bottom anymore, the way he used to. I didn't know if it was a sign of anything, but when he reached out with his hand now, instead of patting he smacked. But I didn't care because I really liked it that way more.

By this time, I was a freshman in high school and getting educated like crazy. I'd finally learned the true meaning of masturbation, and words like lesbian and homosexual didn't throw me anymore. I knew from experience that lesbians made love to each other with their mouths and their hands, but I sure was surprised to find out that some men did the same things. But the only thing that really bothered me was that I couldn't wait

17

to find out what it was like to be a normal female. In school, I'd looked the boys over very carefully to see if I could find one I'd want to get on intimate terms with. From the books I'd sneaked up to my room to read when I was supposed to be asleep, from what Mary Ann had told me, and from what I'd learned the times I'd peeked at Jack with one or another of his girl friends, it seemed to me that fucking was about as intimate as a girl and boy could get. And it looked like a lot more fun than anything I'd ever done. But I hadn't seen a boy I'd allow within finger distance of my pussy, let alone help him get into it with his pecker. From what I could understand, the main difference between fucking and pussy-petting was that for fucking a girl was supposed to feel something before she started. The boys in my school didn't make me feel anything, and I'd convinced myself that when I got out West to the dude ranch Jack was sending me to that summer, I'd be a cinch to meet somebody who got me feeling what I was supposed to be feeling. I sure hoped so. The only man I ever saw who made me feel sort of itchy was Jack, but I didn't dare suggest anything to him, him being just like my father. And I certainly didn't want to wait until I was fourteen or fifteen before I found out what fucking was like. I was sure I'd be nuts about it. Everyone who did it seemed to be. And if I wasn't careful, half my life would be over before I learned to play any sex game but solitaire.

No matter how I tried, I never could find out who sold Jack on the Bar-Nothing Ranch as the perfect place for a thirteen-year-old girl to spend the

18

summer. Every time afterward, whenever I'd bring it up, he'd get a funny look on his face and change the conversation to how I was doing in school, or some other idiotic subject. What possible difference did it make how I was doing in school? I didn't expect to become a space physicist, or any other kind of brain. I was just sort of marking time till I got to be old enough to get out into the world on my own and have a little fun, before I settled down to one guy and started incubating a bunch of babies. But he never would talk about it, and no matter how I pried, he wouldn't open up even a little bit. And actually, after what happened, I really couldn't blame him too much.

It seemed that Jack had gotten together with a brand-new crowd in his social life, and his whole philosophy of girl-raising had been changed. From that far-out bunch of eggheads who believed that anything ought to go, he became chummy with a lot of characters whose ideas went just the other way. They were charter members of the children-should-be-seen-but-not-heard school. I'll say one thing for my Jackson. When he goes for anything, he goes whole-hog. And he started to worry about how I was being equipped to face a world full of chiselers and wolves. What a wonderful dope he is! Here I was, still technically a virgin I suppose, but certainly an old hand at everything else, being wrapped in cotton batting by a man who knew as little about the real me as it was possible for anyone to know. Of course, by this time I'd learned how easy it was to pull the wool over the poor dear's eyes. And I'm sure that if anyone had told him what

19

an experienced veteran I was in certain things, he'd have laughed right in the teller's face.

At this point, the only thing I can think of to say in favor of the old Bar-Nothing is that all of the guests lived in their own private cabins. So I didn't have to worry too much about any nosy characters sticking their two cents into what I did with myself in private. I was more than a little annoyed, though, to find out they had a different set of rules for what they called children than they did for their regular guests. And of course, I was listed as a child. Anyone would think I had to be wet-nursed, fed, bathed, and changed. But that's just one of the burdens a girl of thirteen has to bear. I was considered too young for freedom of action, yet I was too old to have my bottom wiped for me. But everyone has had to live through this time of life, and I just had to put up with it too until a couple of years were added to my age.

Being condemned to the children's section of the ranch, my cabin was a little more secluded than the ones used by the older guests. It was felt that someone like myself required lots of sleep, and if I were too close to the main buildings, the noise of the nightly doings in the lounge might disturb me. What a laugh! But the extra privacy this gave me was something for which I became very grateful. It burned me that I couldn't attend the cocktail parties in the evenings, and that I wasn't allowed to entertain men in my cabin. I was a child and was required to live like one. Plenty of sleep, plenty of food, and plenty of sunshine and fresh air were to be my main activities. Maybe I was only thirteen, but I knew that quite a few of the men vacationers noticed things about me that grown men weren't supposed to notice about little girls. And whenever I got the chance to walk through the lounge in the afternoon, I always wore the tightest jeans I owned, and wiggled my cute little ass for everyone's benefit. It got to be a first-class scandal among the women guests. And finally they raised such a stink about "that little nymphet," the ranch owner, Jim Adams, took me on the side one day and told me that if I didn't stop, he'd apply a paddle to my cute little ass, sans jeans, till I didn't have anything left to wiggle. I guess he wasn't a very progressive-minded man, because he didn't seem at all concerned that the marks this would put on my subconscious would be much more lasting than the ones he'd leave on my bottom. I put on a great act of innocence, insisting I didn't know what he was talking about, but inside I was giggling as hard as I could. It did a lot for my ego to find that even at my age, I could cut those older broads right out of the ball game, with no more than a little wiggle. But Jim had the kind of attitude that made a girl realize he wasn't kidding, so for the sake of protecting my little ass, I stopped wearing jeans and concentrated on showing off my other attributes. I wore tight turtle-neck sleeveless sweaters and the shortest of shorts, and skipped through the lounge bouncing my budding titties. For a while, all the guys sat around making book on how soon my pussy would stick out of those tiny shorts. But pretty soon, all the complaints stopped and I was able to go back to my tight jeans and ass-wiggling routine which I liked much better, because at thirteen it was much sexier looking than the rest of me.

After a few weeks of this kind of thing, I was all

ready to write Jack and ask if I could come back home, when something happened that changed the whole picture of my life. Aggie, the waitress who delivered breakfast to my cabin every morning, came down with some disease that made it necessary for her to go to the hospital. Naturally, I didn't know anything about it because the problems of the help were things I stayed far away from. I figured Jack had put up good money for my comfort, and I was going to get everything that was coming to me. So the next morning I called for my breakfast in the usual way, not realizing my regular waitress was missing.

The first few mornings at the ranch, I was very careful to be wearing my robe when breakfast came. But after several weeks of having it brought by no one but Aggie, I got careless about how I was dressed when I opened the door. On this particular morning, I even unlatched the door before getting into the shower, knowing Aggie would walk right in when she heard the water running in the bathroom. When I was finished in the shower, hearing someone in the bedroom, I waltzed right in, wearing nothing but a comb in one hand, expecting to see Aggie's familiar homely face smiling at me. But there, setting the tray on the table, was the cutest, handsomest, most wonderful-looking male I'd ever seen. He must have been several years older than I. Immediately, I began to get the funniest feeling in the strangest places, the very one I'd been waiting to get from the boys I went to school with. He just stared at me for a minute, his eyes bugging right out of his head. Then he smiled. Were his teeth the whitest! As for me, I'd been raised to be completely unashamed of my body, so instead of letting out a yell and diving back into the bathroom for my robe, I just stood there admiring him from head to foot in exactly the same way he was admiring me. And from the look in his eyes, he seemed to be experiencing the same feeling.

"Hi!" I said casually. "Where's Aggie?"

"Sick."

"Who are you?"

"Red Feather."

"Gosh!" I giggled. "I hated my parents for saddling me with Brittania. Where did you ever get a name like that?"

"What's wrong with it?"

"Nothing . . . I guess."

"It's a good Indian name."

"You a . . . redskin?"

"Cheyenne!" he nodded proudly. "Want me to prove it?"

"You wouldn't . . . scalp me?"

"Naw!"

"Then how?"

"By war whooping."

Somehow I didn't think this was a good idea. The noise would be sure to bring someone nosing around, and I didn't see how I'd be able to explain. Meanwhile, he didn't make any move to leave, even though he'd already delivered my breakfast and I was as naked as the day I was born. I began to feel a strange sensation in my tits as he stared me up and down, the nipples seeming to rise up and stand on end by themselves. It was wonderful. Then I noticed he was standing on end too, in his own masculine way, and I realized he must be new on the job. I'd never seen an Indian naked, or any other way, and suddenly I wanted him more than anything else in the world. I walked

23

over to the bed as casually as I could, wiggling my ass the way I did in the lounge, and sat down facing him, with my legs twisted under me to show off plenty of pussy.

"Red Feather," I said softly. "I'm going to do you a tremendous favor."

He moved a few steps closer to the bed, breathing rapidly, while I pointed to the front of his pants where they were sticking out. "Isn't that uncomfortable?"

"Uh-huh!"

"You better get undressed right away."

"Wha—?"

"Naked!" I ordered, enjoying my new role as a Madame du Barry. "That is . . . if you're interested in some paleface pussy."

"What if I am interested?"

"You better be, because I'm a virgin. And I want to get fucked, the first time, by an Indian —a full-blooded Cheyenne Indian."

Dropping his pants and shirt where he stood, and stepping right out of his moccasins, he made a flying leap through the air, landing right on top of me and flattening me on the bed, his hands coming to rest on my tits, his lips on my mouth, and his pecker, as rigid as a flagpole, resting between my thighs. Indian fashion, he began slithering about on my body, kissing my mouth, my tits, and my pussy, almost at one and the same time, he changed positions so quickly. Then he turned me over underneath him and started biting at my bottom, real hard. The first time I felt the nip of his teeth, I started to squeal. But right away I found that I liked it, so instead of yelling I giggled.

In spite of all my pussy-petting and playing

24

with other girls, I was pretty much of an innocent when it came to girl-boy love-making. But what I lacked in experience, I more than made up for in activity. I grabbed for his pecker, first squeezing it gently, and then planting little kisses all along its length. He seemed to like this attention, groaning and moaning with pleasure.

Finally, hoisting me roughly until I was resting on my hands and knees, he jumped behind me and shoved his swollen pecker into me with a quick hard push. Gosh it hurt! But almost at once this stopped, and it began to feel wonderful as he moved his flagpole in and out, slowly and gently. After a few minutes of this, he picked up speed, and pretty soon he was banging away at me like a locomotive. I didn't have to do anything but feel and enjoy. Then, it almost seemed like a miracle, we both exploded at the same time and collapsed on the bed with a lot of shuddering, me on my face with Red Feather on top, breathing and sighing in the same way Jack had when I used to watch him doing this with his girl friends. But I didn't feel a bit like sighing. I felt more like yelling. This was wonderful! It was the greatest! I always knew I'd be crazy about doing it once I had the chance to try, and I was in a tearing hurry to try it again.

When I asked Red Feather why he did it from such a funny position, he said that it was the true Cheyenne dog-style position, and it was how the braves of his tribe always started virgins. Then I asked him how long it would be till we could do it again, and he said he would be ready whenever I was. Only this time, we'd do it the white man's way, me on my back with him on top of me. As I held his pecker in my hand, it began to stand up again. And before it could change its mind, we eased it in and started banging away. I liked this position better, with the man looking at my face instead of my bottom, and I got myself ready for another explosion.

But this time it didn't have such a happy ending. The cook had begun worrying about why it was taking Red Feather so long to come back. With Aggie sick, he'd figured it was safe to send the Indian boy because I was only a child. And busybody that he was, he sent Patsy, another of the waitresses, to find out if anything was wrong. Right in the middle of one of Red Feather's pushes, she came barging into the cabin without even knocking. Seeing what was going on, she let out a scream and jumped on the bed with us, trying to get us apart. But Red Feather and I had our legs about each other, and we resisted as strongly as we could. In the middle of our struggling, Patsy began yelling for help as loudly as she could, and pretty soon the little cabin was crammed full of people, Jim Adams among them, all of them pulling and tugging to get Red Feather and me apart. And after a regular tug-of-war, they succeeded.

The women were screaming that the two of us ought to be horsewhipped off the ranch, but most of the men just stood around snickering, and eyeing Red Feather with a little envy. But at Jim's orders, the poor boy, as naked as when Patsy had found us, was hauled out and locked in one of the stables to wait for the sheriff. Then, with his eyes shooting fire at me, Jim told me he was going to call Jack and have him come and take me off his ranch forever. He said that in the few weeks I'd been there, I'd already caused more trouble among the guests than anyone else had in fourteen years. But before he called, he was going to demonstrate how thirteen-year-olds who were too big for their britches ought to be treated. Before I knew what he had in mind, me having been raised in an atmosphere in which free expression was the thing, he had me face down across his lap and was smacking the devil out of my bare bottom in front of everybody. It didn't take any time at all before I was bawling like a calf with a branding iron stuck up its ass, but he kept at it for a good while. Then he locked me in the cabin and went off to place his call to Jack.

The two days I spent in my cabin at the Bar-Nothing, till Jack arrived to take me back home, were almost the most awful I can remember. I stayed inside the cabin because I couldn't get out. I was locked in, and my food was brought to me three times a day by Jim Adams himself. I guess after what happened he didn't trust anyone else in the place with me. Which was probably just as well, because from what I could overhear through the windows, the rest of the help, especially the waitresses, were very much concerned about Red Feather's future. He seemed to be a great favorite with them, for reasons with which I would be forced to agree. And if they'd found themselves alone with me inside that cabin, they'd probably have whacked me better than Jim did, just for kicks.

But even the sight of Jim was enough to make my hair stand on end. Everytime I heard his key rattling in the lock, I'd back into a corner like a cat ready to spit, watching him carefully and waiting for him to put down the tray and get out. I wouldn't talk to him, and absolutely refused to answer any of his questions. If, a couple of times, I started to feel a little less hostile toward him, all I had to do was press my hind end up against the wall to remember how he'd spanked it in front of everybody, and I'd get teed-off at him all over again. That had been the first time in my life anyone had really hit me, and I was positively shaken at the weird-looking marks his hand had left on my bottom. They were frightening, and the first thing I did, when Jack showed up, was to drop my jeans and show him what Jim had done to me. Up to then, Jack, too, had been pretty mad at me, though he was convinced none of it had really been my fault. He'd put the whole blame on Jim and the ranch for allowing a wild Indian to come into the cabin of a young and innocent girl all by himself. But the minute he saw my condition, he rushed me into my clothes and off to the airport, as if the whole Cheyenne Nation was howling after our scalps. Actually, it looked worse than it hurt. But I didn't let on because I found it was a wonderful way to get Jack to do whatever I wanted. A tear or two, with my hands pressed tenderly against the back of my panties, and I was home free. But while he was convinced I was still an innocent child and not to blame for anything that had happened, I couldn't talk him out of his decision to ship me off to some fancy finishing school, where the progressive educational attitudes of the faculty would allow my personality to flower to the fullest, without my being intimidated physically, or forced into a pattern of behavior by the old-fashioned methods of a brute like Jim Adams. Besides, he was scared to death that a little bastard half-breed might show up on the scene as a result of Red Feather's intimate attentions, and he didn't want me in town where everyone could notice. Which is why I found myself, about two weeks later, having lunch in a chic restaurant with Jack and a prissy-faced broad named Millicent Bullfinch. She was the head mistress at Revere Hall, a school for young ladies, in some jerkwater town called Cherry Hills, a description that would never again fit my physical person.

Jack had already given the old hag a rundown on my past performances, and she was gushing all over me in what she thought was a great job of making me feel at ease. She was one of those nuts who really thought it was dangerous to travel west of the Alleghenies because of Indians and buffalo stampedes. I felt a little sorry for her because she had as much chance of making friends with me as a rock 'n' roll group did of playing a convention of nuns. I watched her vomity performance quietly, waiting for a chance to let a little of the air out of her well-filled belly. The way she was going at it, she wouldn't even miss it. She slobbered over Jack disgustingly, describing all the advantages her "dear girls" enjoyed at the school. She went on and on about her job being only to nurture delicate plants, not to force them into predetermined patterns, but to guide their natural progress. Limiting imagination and the free expression of youth would be a crime. But I'd already made up my mind she wasn't going to add me to her collection of "dear girls" if there was anything I could do to prevent it.

"It's frightening," the Big Wind simpered at

Jack, while she ate like there was no tomorrow, "what unfeeling people put young girls through these days. They've lost the realization these delicate children are like fresh lovely buds in the spring. If one petal is damaged, the scar will remain forever in the full-grown flower. If allowed to fester, this sort of hurt can infect a girl's entire subconscious."

"I agree completely, Miss Bullfinch." My rock-headed guardian spooned up all that crap as if it were whipped cream. "That's why I'm so anxious to help Brick forget the whole horrible experience."

"She's fortunate to have as understanding a guardian as you, Mr. Brant," the old hag said. "After her frightening experience—actually the most terrible a young girl can undergo . . . being assaulted by an aborigine—to beat this fragile child as if she were an animal! Why, it's unbelievable! Simply unbelievable! Any man who did that ought to be horsewhipped!"

"I agree."

"How do you feel about it, my dear?" she turned her sickly smile on me.

"I don't really know, Miss Bullfinch," I muttered, fooling around with the food on my plate. "But . . . I want to do the right thing . . . now!"

"You'll be doing that at Revere Hall," simpered Windy. "I think your guardian is making a wise decision for you. And don't you worry, my dear. We'll help you to forget."

"Do you think I can?" I wailed brokenly on the outside while snickering inside.

"I'm sure you can."

"M-m-may I . . . ask you something?"

"Of course, my dear. Anything."

30

"Do the girls do much pussy-petting up at the Hall?"

"Oh, I'm sorry," she shook her head sadly. "But pets aren't allowed on the school grounds. But is there anything else I can tell you?"

"Yes. Have you ever been fucked by an Indian?"

In the thirty seconds of dead silence that followed, Miss Bullfinch's sallow complexion reflected all the colors of the rainbow, ending up bright red. "Oh, m-my d-d-dear," she stammered, trying very hard to smile.

Jack reached over quickly and grabbed my hand in a tight grip, squeezing hard to show me he suspected what I was doing, and warning me to cut it out if he was right. But I worked my hand free of his and turned back toward Miss Bullfinch with eagerness. She mistook my interest for anxiety and placed her hand gently on Jack's arm as a sign for him to allow her to handle the problem.

"Well? Have you?" I insisted.

"Of course not," shuddered the old bag, but I couldn't tell whether it was from gratitude or disappointment. "But you must not allow the horror of it to color your whole existence. Try to forget."

I managed to squeeze a tear from my eyes. "I can't," I wailed. "I'll never be able to forget."

"Hush, my dear," Miss Bullfinch comforted me, her eyes shining with excitement for the future. "When we're up at the school together, you can tell me all about it."

"But I don't want to wait till then," I cried loudly, adding a few sobs just for effect. "I want to tell you now. You're such a wonderful person . . . almost like a m-mother!"

"Brick!" Jack whispered angrily, completely sure

31

by now that I was putting on an act. "Cut it out, damn it!"

Everyone in the restaurant had heard me and was staring toward our table with interest. Ignoring Jack, I turned again to Miss Bullfinch and began to rant in an unnecessarily loud voice. "Oh, it was awful! It was awful! I'll never be able to forget it! Every night I can see that slimy fat pecker in my dreams. It's always fiery red! You said you'd never been fucked by an Indian so you can't imagine what it was like! When he took off his clothes it hung way down below his knees. It fascinated me just like a snake. I couldn't move and I couldn't get away. Then it started growing. It grew till it stuck out like a flagpole . . . out to here! He threw me on the bed and . . . when he pushed that big thing into my little pussy . . . oh, it was awful!"

The maître d'hôtel, several of the waiters, and two of the busboys came running over to our table. But the more everyone tried to shush me, the more I raised my voice. I shook my finger in a cringing Miss Bullfinch's face. "It's easy for you to tell me to forget. You've never been fucked by an Indian. The way you talk I don't think you've ever been fucked by anyone . . . you old biddy!"

"Brick!" Jack yelled. "Stop that right away!"

"What can a dried-up old fink like you do to help me?" I shouted at the horribly embarrassed woman. "What do you know about fucking? Imagine you trying to act like you don't know what pussy-petting means. You've probably been doing it every night for sixty years, you frustrated old bitch!"

Now that she was on the pan, the saccharine façade was quickly stripped from Miss Bullfinch's face, leaving it the mean, hard face of a spiteful old maid. She jumped to her feet like she'd been goosed out of her chair, waving her pocketbook like it was a bludgeon. "To think I was considering you for a place at Revere Hall," she shrieked.

"I couldn't stand the stink of the place if it has any more old pussies like you in it," I screamed back.

"I wouldn't be surprised if you didn't seduce that Indian, you little monster," she spat at me. "It's a wonder you didn't tear the genitals right off him while you were at it. You don't need a finishing school. You need to be sent to reform school where they'd beat you every day—whether you deserved it or not!"

"Miss Bullfinch!" Jack gulped with shock. "You assured me you didn't believe in beating children. What about the bud . . . and the injury to the petal?"

"You lock me in a room with that filthy-mouthed devil and I'll injure her buds till she can't sit on them for a month! She's the most unspeakable little tart I've ever seen in my life!"

The maître d'hôtel had by this time grabbed Jack by the collar. One of the waiters now took me under the arms, while another seized Miss Bullfinch before she had a real foaming fit, and the three of us were rushed out into the street. Then, standing in the entrance, the poor man pointed his finger at Jack and told him that the restaurant would be closed to him as long as he continued as maître d'hôtel. Miss Bullfinch had twisted her knee coming through the door, and was running down the street, crying, limping, and looking like an old drunk in her cups. I just leaned up against the front of the building and howled

33

with laughter till Jack flagged down a cab and shoved me into it.

I'd never seen Jack as teed-off at me as he was when we got home after that crazy lunch with Miss Bullfinch. He'd had such great hopes for me from it, and all it had turned out to be was a complete disaster. I guess what made it even worse was his knowing I'd torpedoed it deliberately. For a while, I thought he might go primitive and wallop my back end himself. And it didn't make me feel any better to hear Wong How, our Chinese house-boy who'd helped raise me since I'd first come to live with Jack, recommending this strongly. But the poor guy chickened out when he came face to face with the actual doing. And instead, he satisfied his conscience by locking me in my room for a whole week.

Looking back at it now, I'm a little bit sorry he was such a piss-willy. It might have saved me a lot of time and trouble. Not that I'd have enjoyed his whacking me. But the way I'd always felt about him, and the way I hoped he could feel about me, he just might have developed a couple of different notions when he had me stretched out across his lap, with my bottom end cleared for action. And I'd have been willing to take that chance. I've always been a very big reader, and I've read this has been known to happen when the girl involved is interested in the man as a man, and the man is interested in the girl the same way, even if he hasn't gotten around to realizing it as yet. Oh, I know Jack loved me all right, but strictly as a cute little nuisance, not as a woman. And it never occurred to him that I could be look-

34

ing for more than a fatherly pat, a kiss on the fore-head, and money for the movies.

But instead, he showed up in my room a week later, and told me he had made an appointment for me with a Dr. Freund, who was going to try to straighten me out. When I said I never felt better in my life, Jack said this doctor didn't treat ordinary, everyday diseases. His work was entirely with the mind, him being a psychiatrist, and he'd told Jack I sounded like an interesting and cura-ble case, after hearing what I'd done.

Actually, I was thrilled. What a status symbol. Imagine! Being the patient of a regular psychia-trist at my age. This would knock the kids I went to school with right off their rockers. Not that I really needed a psychiatrist. I knew that the only thing wrong with me was that, though I was still rather young, I was mature for my age, and terri-bly in love with my guardian. After all, he was only thirty-eight, and everything I did was to get him to notice me as a woman. I didn't know how else to do it. But that didn't mean I was going to bare my all to any head-shrinker. So I kept my face straight, while giggling a little inside, at the stories I'd make up for that medical square. When he got through with me, or better yet, when I got through with him, he'd be the one who needed help. And all through breakfast I kept rehearsing how I'd act, since my first appointment was for eleven that very morning.

I have to admit I was terribly disappointed in Dr. Freund's office, and in the man himself. In my imagination, I pictured an exotically furnished place, with thick carpets, black satin drapes to

35

shut out the light whenever some self-conscious female wanted to be extra-confidential, and a sexy dream of a couch. I'd heard a lot of talk about what sometimes happened on those couches, and I was really dying to see one up close. But the doctor turned out to be a fat, sloppy little guy with a bald head, a tic in one eye, and a beard that looked like a family of moths lived in it. And his office was a positive disgrace, at least to me. Messy and dusty, there wasn't any kind of couch for me to lie down on when he got the yen to dive into my subconscious. All I could see was a desk, a chair for himself and one for the patient, an open file cabinet, and a tape recorder. Recorders always fascinated me. But when I asked him what this one was for, he rudely told me to shut up—he was paid to ask the questions.

I'd been a little leery of this doctor before I'd even seen him, because of the frightening reputation psychiatrists have for braininess. But in the beginning, he almost scared me to death. Jack had warned me he might be a bit eccentric. Yet for no reason that I could see, he'd get a strange look in his eyes, jump up and down, and start waving his fists in the air like a maniac. After he'd done it a few times, I asked him whether anything was wrong. But he just mumbled something about oversexed, nosy little twots, and told me to shut up again.

I wasn't sure whether he had all his marbles or not, but just to be on the safe side, I figured I'd better sit quietly and wait for him to make the first move. Suddenly, without any warning, he started firing questions at me. At first, they didn't make much sense—at least, considering why I had come to see him. But I figured if Jack wanted to waste his money, it was O.K. with me. What was my favorite color? Did I like going to school? What was my ambition in life? Then, he asked me if I enjoyed being in the same classroom with boys. When I assured him I did, he wanted to know if I'd ever tried to sneak into the boys' rest room when nobody was looking. That burned me up and I started to get mad. But before I could say anything, he jumped up, came around the desk, and asked me very confidentially how many times a week I masturbated. Well, now it was time to have a little fun. So I just stared at him blankly.

"What does that mean?" I asked.

"What?"

"That word you just used?"

"Masturbation?"

"That's it."

"You don't know what masturbation means . . . at your age?"

"No."

"Do you know how to agitate your clitoris?"

"I don't think so. I didn't even know I had one."

"Do you know what you have between your legs?"

"Nothing," I said, looking down at them.

"I think you'd better get undressed. I'm going to have to explain a few things to you," he muttered.

"Undressed? Right here?"

"Where else?"

"How much do you want me to take off?"

"Everything!"

"Gosh!" I said. "Jack told me you were just a head doctor."

"Top or bottom, I'm a doctor. And there's nothing for you to be embarrassed about. I've seen plenty of naked girls before."

"Oh, I'm not embarrassed," I smiled. "Did you like them?"

"Who?"

"Those naked girls you looked at?"

"I didn't look at them the way you mean. Anyway, we're not here to discuss my peculiarities. Just yours."

"That's funny! I don't jump up and down and wave my fists in the air at nothing."

"Perhaps. But I don't jump in the hay with wild Indians, either."

"Red Feather wasn't wild. He was kind and gentle."

"O.K. He was a knight in shining armor—without any armor," he shrugged. "But why did you act the way you did with that schoolteacher?"

"I didn't like her."

"But you liked the redskin, huh?"

"He was the greatest!"

Suddenly, Dr. Freund jumped up and down like crazy, waving his fists wildly over his head. "Why do you do that?" I asked, after he'd calmed down.

"It relaxes me."

"That's just what Red Feather did for me."

"You liked what he did to you?"

"I loved it."

"Then he didn't force you?"

"Certainly not. I only wish he were here so he could relax me the same way all the time."

"You'd probably kill him off in a month. Did he make you pregnant too?"

"No. Everything came through right on time . . . last week."

"You're a lucky little nympho. Now strip!"

38

I started undressing slowly, trying to remember everything I'd once read in an article by Gypsy Rose Lee, about the proper way to undress in front of a husband. Not that this nutty character was my husband, thank God! But still, he was a man, and this seemed like too good an opportunity to pass up. But I must have forgotten some of the more important steps, because instead of desire, the only thing that showed on his face was impatience. He even looked at his watch a couple of times, which made me feel very insulted. Finally, when he couldn't stand my dawdling any longer, he reached out, grabbed the top of my panties, and yanked them down below my knees. Ignoring his bad manners, I stepped out of them as casually as if I undressed in front of strange men all the time. Then, I moved away a couple of steps and did a sort of pirouette, to show myself off from every angle.

"Well?" I asked. "What do you think?"

"About what?"

"About me."

"I think you look like a young girl without any clothes on," he said, eying me coolly from top to bottom. "Also, a little like a young snot trying to act grown-up."

"You're a very rude man," I said, quickly moving closer until I was standing directly in front of him. "What did you want to explain to me?"

"This!" And before I realized what he was doing, he reached out and pushed his hand between my legs, grabbing himself a handful of hair.

"Ow!" I yelped. "That hurts!"

"Then stop phutzing around and pay attention. Do you know what this is?"

"Of course! It's my pussy!"

"Do you ever play with it?"

"Is that what that word means?" I asked innocently.

"That's what it means."

"Well, my God! If you're talking about pussy-petting, it's a pity you wouldn't say so."

"Well, do you?"

"Do I what?"

"Pussy-pet?"

"For years . . . ever since Mary Ann taught me how."

"Who's she?"

"A counselor at the camp I used to go to when I was a child."

"Did she help you do it often?"

"Every chance she had. But she couldn't help it. She had a thing for me. She was a les."

While we were talking, he kept his hand on my pussy. I didn't try to push it away, because I didn't know what scientific medical experiment he had in mind. After a few minutes, he began to move his hand around, examining the area slowly.

"My!" he muttered. "You've got the compression chamber of a woman ten years your senior." And continuing with his testing, he pushed his little finger inside me, wiggling it about like a worm on a fishhook. "Is this how she taught you?"

"Hmmm . . . yes!"

"You like?"

"I like!"

Then, for no reason at all, he started to take his hand away. But after what he'd begun, I wasn't about to have any of that. And closing my thighs as tightly as I could, I kept his hand trapped between my legs, pressed firmly up against my pussy. He stared at me with surprise.

40

"Oh? Real itchy, huh?"

"Uh-huh!"

"I don't approve of this," he said.

"Why?"

"Because this is something every girl ought to do for herself. But . . ."

Dropping into the chair I'd been sitting on when I first came in, he eased me onto his lap and finished what he had started with his examination. I had my arms wrapped around his neck, and even though I kept moving my bottom back and forth across his crotch, I couldn't feel any signs of activity beneath me at all.

"You a zombi?" I asked, staring at him wonderingly.

"Why?"

"You've got me naked . . . on your lap . . . with your hand up my pussy, and your pecker doesn't seem to know anything about it!"

I guess that was the wrong thing to say, because I'd no sooner finished than he jumped to his feet, sending me sprawling, bare as I was, toward the floor. But as nutty as he was, he couldn't have known that my head would bang into the side of the desk, leaving me stretched out unconscious on the floor.

How long I was out I don't know, but when I came to, I was still naked, and still stretched out, but now, on a long, low table in a little room off the doctor's office. Through the slightly open door, I could hear the steady murmur of voices, both of them masculine, and one of them definitely belonging to the psychiatrist. Ignoring the pounding in my head, and sliding off the table as quietly as I could, I tiptoed to the door and peeked through the narrow opening. I could just

41

see Dr. Freund and a strange man, both of them as naked as I was, tossing something at each other. I opened the door another inch or two, to get a better look. Each of these characters had an impressive-looking erection, and was concentrating on trying to throw a ringer over the other's pecker with the largest doughnut I'd even seen. As soon as one made it, he'd run over, grab back the doughnut, and eat it. Then they'd take a fresh one from the bag on the desk and start all over again. This was too good to miss. And pushing the door completely open, I strolled casually into the other room, disregarding the fact that the three of us were stark naked.

"Is this a private hootenanny, fellows?" I asked hopefully. "Or can anybody get into it?"

Looking back at everything now, I can understand how sometimes the tiniest thing will have the greatest effect on a person's life. If my guardian, Jack, wasn't such a handsome and exciting bachelor, he probably wouldn't have been running around with a bunch of oversexed females who wanted me out from underfoot, and I'd never have been sent to Camp Winnepesaukee in the first place. And if I hadn't, I'd never have met Mary Ann and become such an expert at pussy-petting, and I wouldn't have developed my terrific yen to try everything else so young. I'd never have talked Jack into sending me out West to the Bar-Nothing Ranch, I wouldn't have met Red Feather, and I wouldn't have been able to seduce him into banging me Cheyenne style. Then, of course, I wouldn't have had to rile up old lady Bullfinch the way I did, making Jack send me to a psychiatrist. And if I hadn't become Dr. Freund's patient, he'd never have been able to introduce me into the Committee for a Sane Universe. So the big brain who first said that the shape of the world's future can usually be traced directly back to the shape of some female's ass end certainly knew his onions. Because it was at a meeting of the Committee that I first ran across Benjy. And I know I'd never even have heard of him if some hustling tomato, back when I was nine years old, hadn't developed a fire in her box that could only be extinguished by Jack's pecker, and didn't want a curious little girl watching her every movement. Because no matter how free and easy a chick might be about showing off her merchandise, she always does her sincerest fucking in private. And it's tough to get your heart and soul into it when some little busybody keeps sticking her runny nose into what doesn't concern her.

After that first time at Dr. Freund's, when I came in and interrupted his game of ring-around-the-flagpole, I remained his steady patient for better than a year and a half, or until I was past fifteen. Twice every week I visited his office, never missing a single appointment. Jack, of course, figured the little guy was a miracle-worker because of the way he seemed to have straightened me out, and worth every cent of his twenty-five-dollar-a-session fee. What the poor dear didn't know, and never found out, was that my obedience to Dr. Freund had nothing to do with my being straightened out. It was all built on sex. But, unfortunately, it was the kind of sex that had nothing to do with fucking. Other than for my experience with Red Feather, and one torrid bout with the doctor, I still was strictly a pussy-petter. It wasn't that I wanted to be. I just never ran across another opportunity to do anything else. In spite of all the talk about the wildness of my generation, and its complete lack of moral values, the boys I met were such drips, they didn't understand too much about what to do with their peckers. I guess most of them considered them to be purely ornamental. And after trying as hard as I could to get Dr. Freund interested in a little medicinal ucking-fe, I came to the conclusion I was a washout where sex appeal was concerned. Each time I went to his office those first weeks, I'd find an excuse for undressing, so he could make an intimate examination of me. But he might just as well have been made of wood for all the effect it had on him. I'd develop a pain high up on the inside of my thigh, or complain of a strange sensation on my bottom. In six weeks, I spent more time naked in his presence than I ever did in my own bedroom. But after he'd examined me from every angle, and in a few positions I hadn't been familiar with before, I figured that as a femme fatale, I was a complete bust. Up till then, the only time I'd ever seen the doctor with an erection was when I busted into his crazy little game of ringers with that other man, who, incidently, I never saw again. And no matter how I wiggled my hips, inside my clothes or out, or how I rubbed my bottom against him, I aroused about as much reaction in him as a piece of raw liver.

Then, one day when I was going through my usual routine for his benefit, he told me I was wasting my time because he was a type of odd-ball. But when I asked him what that meant, he shook his head as if he didn't believe me.

"You take the cake," he laughed.

44

"Why?"

"Don't you know what an oddball is?"

"No!"

"For a female who suffers from clitoral stimulation as much as you do, you're strangely ignorant. But then, you told me the same thing once about masturbation. Yet you turned out to be a major leaguer at it."

"That's because I don't always understand your technical language," I insisted. "If you'd use plain everyday words, maybe I'd know what you were talking about."

"I suppose you mean the sort of words that are written on the walls of public toilets."

"At least I know what they mean."

"Do you know what homosexuals are?"

"Of course. They're people who like to play around with their own kind."

"That's right."

"O.K. Then what's an oddball?"

"Sort of the same thing . . . in a way."

"You mean you don't like to . . . fuck?"

"Not according to accepted methods."

"I thought everybody did. Gosh! That's terrible."

"Why?"

"Look at all the fun you're missing!"

"What makes you say that?"

"Gosh! Don't you ever get the yen to slide your plow handle into a nice warm tight slippery place, and bang hips with the girl till you both explode?"

"No."

"Not even dog-style?"

"What's dog-style?"

"The Cheyenne way of breaking in virgins."

"Who told you that?"

"Red Feather."

"Oh! That sexy Indian of yours, huh?"

"Yes."

"For the length of time you two were together, he seems to have provided you with an extensive education along certain lines."

"He was terrific."

"He must have been. And you haven't forgotten him."

"How can I? After all, he was my first."

"Who was your second?" the doctor asked curiously.

"No one," I muttered. "I hoped you'd be but I can't seem to get you interested."

"I'm a psychiatrist, Brick. Not a stud!"

"But you're giving me an inferiority complex!" I cried, tears starting to trickle down my cheeks. "You're supposed to help me, not break me down."

"How am I breaking you down?"

"You refuse to notice me . . . as a woman!"

"Oh, I notice you as a woman, all right. You're remarkably pretty, your breasts are beautifully formed, your legs are terrific, and your hips are delightful."

"They are?"

"They sure are!"

I jumped up and ran around the desk quickly, throwing myself on his lap, before he could change his mind. "Then . . . why don't you do something about all of them?"

"What do you want me to do?"

"You never even offered to play a game with me," I muttered.

"What kind of game?"

"Like the one you played with that man the first time I came here."

"You can't play that. You're missing part of the equipment."

"I could wear something."

"Don't be childish! I've got something serious to say to you."

"What?"

"I want you to promise to stop trying to have intercourse with every man you meet . . . at least until you are married."

"Gosh! That might be a long time."

"Somehow I don't think it will take as long as you do," smiled the doctor.

"O.K.," I shrugged. "But that means I'll have to go right on pussy-petting."

"Why not? It's much safer—and just as satisfying."

"But . . . there's no one to talk to!"

"So what? You can't ever get pregnant, or catch any diseases either."

"What kind of diseases?"

"Syphilis, gonorrhea, and things like that."

"You mean it's healthier for me to pussy-pet than to fuck?"

"It is . . . until you're married."

"Then why is everybody so secretive about it? Hardly anyone likes to admit doing it. Even Mary Ann refused to talk about it in front of strangers."

"You admit it."

"I wasn't talking about me, but about all the others I know who do it. They'd rather die than say so."

"Only because they're stupid and ignorant," said Dr. Freund. "They're products of a stupid and unimaginative culture. If everyone would just have the good sense to play with themselves, or masturbate, now that you know what the word

47

means, single girls would never get caught, venereal diseases would die out in one generation, and most of the sexual scandal in the world would never take place. There wouldn't be any bastards, either."

"Why?"

"Because single people would refuse to have intercourse with a member of the opposite sex. The essential thing, in order for a woman to get pregnant, is for male sperm cells to contact her monthly egg."

"I never thought of that. Gosh! Then all the years I've been pussy-petting, I've actually been doing a service for mankind!"

"Correct!"

"Gee! I can't wait to get home so I can tell Jack!"

"Don't you dare!" Dr. Freund ordered sternly.

"Why not?"

"He'd probably have me arrested!"

"But why? Don't you believe what you're telling me?"

"Of course I believe it! But others aren't intelligent enough to understand. And until they are, people like you and me will just have to do our good work for mankind in secret. I'm sure your guardian would be furious with me. And you, too. From what you've told me about him, he's a pretty active cocksman. And those fellows consider it a crime to waste a drop."

"Do you ever pussy-pet?" I asked slowly.

"How can I?"

"That's right. You don't have one, do you?"

"No."

"But what do you do? You aren't married, either."

48

"I play games like ring-around-the-penis with other men who think the way I do."

"Don't say that!" I begged.

"What?"

"Penis."

"Why not?"

"I like the word pecker much better."

"But penis is the correct term for the male organ."

"I don't care. When a man has an erection, and it bounces up and down when he walks around, it looks just like a rooster about to peck at something."

"How do you know so much about it?"

"Because I'm experienced. I've fucked already and you haven't."

"Who told you that?"

"You did."

"I did not! All I said was I'm a breed of oddball. I used to have intercourse with girls all the time when I was going to college. But finally I became worried about the future of our culture, and I reached the point where I didn't think the risk was worth the pleasure. So I turned to other things."

"Do you have as much fun now?"

"More! Now I don't have to be concerned about anything but myself."

"I'm sure you're probably right," I muttered. "But I wish you'd fuck me just once so I'd have something to hold onto till I do get married."

"If I do, Brick, will you promise to stop dreaming about doing it all the time, and stick to masturbation until you can start copulating with your own husband?"

"What's copulating?"

"Fucking."

"I promise!"

Dr. Freund never wanted to talk to me about what happened next as long as I remained his patient, a time that stretched on for almost a year and a half more. And, of course, I've never laid eyes on him since. All I can figure is that he didn't enjoy himself too much, in spite of his saying he was a perfectly normal male, who'd only turned from girls to oddballing because he was terribly worried about the culture, the morality, and the future of a disease-free mankind. As for me, though, while it was rougher than I expected, I thought it was simply great. I guess it only goes to prove you can never judge a person by looks alone. So I could say, that along with the fun, it was a real educational experience for me. And though I wouldn't admit it even under torture, the little guy turned out to be an awful lot better than Red Feather. I suppose his greater age and training had a good deal to do with his performance, because my Indian lover had been only a boy himself. And while he tried to satisfy the sex urges of the unattached waitresses at the Bar-Nothing, an odd squaw or two, and as many of the ranch's female guests as were interested in exploring native American culture, he didn't have the same sophisticated approach. His racial background, being more primitive, he was much more direct. And, believe me, it showed up in the action.

The first thing Dr. Freund did was warn me very definitely to be prepared for anything, because as an oddballer with a completely scientific psychiatric approach, his actions might take off in any direction. And as long as I had asked for it, I had to be ready for any consequences that developed. Of course I agreed right away. By this time, I had such a yen and a fire in my pussy, I didn't care what happened as long as he made like a fireman and put the darn thing out.

He led me into a little room off his office, the same one in which I'd found myself, on my first visit, after being knocked unconscious by hitting my head against his desk. He told me to get undressed while he dragged out of the closet an inflatable mattress and a horse's tail on a cord. I was a bit surprised but I didn't say anything because I could hardly wait to get started. When I was naked, he tied the tail around, adjusting it against my bottom until it looked as if it had actually grown on me. As a matter of fact, I twisted my hips a few times and heehawed, and was tickled to see it acted like the real thing. Then, he took off his own clothes, hung them in the closet along with mine, and brought out a little toy-like switch, which he attached to his wrist with a loop. Forcing me onto my hands and knees, he mounted me as if he were riding a horse. Grabbing a handful of my hair for reins, he ordered me to start running around the room. I started to move very carefully because I wasn't sure if he could stay on my back, and I certainly didn't want him to fall off and hurt himself before we even started. But it wasn't fast enough for him. And lifting up the tail, he gave me a quick hard cut across my bottom with the tiny switch. It felt like the sting of a hundred bees.

"Ow!" I screamed. "What are you doing?"

"Teaching a young filly who's boss," he said.

And just to show he wasn't fooling, he hit me twice more, harder than before.

That started it, the nuttiest bareback ride I was to have for some time. Scared half to death by the stinging, I began running around the room on my hands and knees, with Dr. Freund hanging on, whipping my bottom at each step, and shouting "Tallyho!" at the top of his lungs. He did a pretty good job on me, too. Because later, when everything was all over and I had backed up to a mirror to inspect the damage, there were more red lines crisscrossing my bottom than there was white skin. In a couple of minutes, it hurt so much I just had to cry. But he kept it up until I collapsed exhausted on the floor, unable to move another inch in spite of the terrible whipping he gave my poor bottom. When he finally realized I couldn't go any further, and he became tired of whipping me and yelling "Tallyho," he threw the switch into the corner, dragged me over to the mattress, turned me on my back, and flopped down alongside me.

I was gasping for breath and sobbing and gulping, but I was so scared I just lay there without saying anything, with my bottom even more on fire than my pussy. Then he started kissing each of my nipples until they stood almost straight up in the air, and stroking my pussy with a gentle motion. Suddenly I was so burning all over, front and back, I could hardly wait for him to push his pecker into me.

It's a good thing he was a scientific man. Being a doctor, and my doctor in the bargain, he couldn't afford to take any chances by exploding inside of me. I was too far along to care. But he managed to remember that if he got me pregnant, Jack would run him out of the country. So keeping it up until he made me explode three times, he pulled out quickly and collapsed on top of me, his pecker pressed between us, spurting its warm, sticky fluid all over my belly up to my breasts. Right away, he rolled off and fell into a deep sleep that must have lasted ten minutes, while I just lay stretched out on the mattress, completely relaxed and feeling sorry for the way he had tired himself out. Finally, he woke up and looked over at me with a smile.

"Satisfied?" he asked.

"Uh-huh!"

"Now don't forget your promise, Brick. That has to last you till you're married."

"I know," I sighed. "But . . ."

"What?"

"There's one thing I don't understand."

"What's that?"

I started to edge closer to him, but the rubbing of the mattress against my whipped bottom made it start to burn all over again. "Ouch!" I muttered, easing myself down next to him.

"What's wrong?"

"My b-b-bottom! It h-hurts t-t-terribly!"

"I warned you before we started," he said, lifting himself onto his elbows. "But don't worry. It'll stop hurting in a little while, and pretty soon, it'll be as good as new again."

"Gosh! I hope so! I'd hate to have to explain to Jack why I can't sit down. But . . ."

"But what?"

"Do you do that often?"

"What?"

"Ride a girl . . . and whip her . . . like a horse?"

"I haven't in years. But it made me feel like a college boy again."

"Is that part of oddballing, or is it just the pulling out and leaking all over my belly?"

"The pulling out was for your protection and mine. I don't think I'd like explaining to your guardian how you became pregnant. And the riding bit isn't really oddballing. That was just something left over from my school days. At the last minute I remembered about the horse's tail and the toy whip I'd hidden away in the closet. Did you enjoy it?"

"Oh, it was wonderful!" I sighed. "Even though the whipping did make me cry. But . . . how did you ever think of it in the first place?"

"That was what originally got me interested in psychiatry," said the doctor. "I used to run around with a cute little girl at college who taught it to me. She was a real nympho, but she was scared to death of getting pregnant. It seems she had an older sister who died in childbirth, and it left her with a fear of having children. So she'd never allow any boy to penetrate her vagina with his penis. Instead, she'd make her dates ride her like a horse and whip her into a frenzy. Then she'd have an orgasm and be completely satisfied. Of course, it was a little hard on her buttocks, but she didn't seem to mind."

"What about her dates?" I asked curiously. "What did they do?"

"Oh, she'd finish a fellow up by hand. And when he was ready to ejaculate, she'd point his penis at her belly button and take his charge all over her. That used to thrill her too. Said it made her feel all warm and womanly. I used to think she was crazy at first, but it started me thinking

54

how much safer her system was than copulating. Since the penis never contacted the vagina, there was absolutely no danger of disease, and no chance for accidental pregnancy. And it made me realize how much better off the world would be, physically and morally, if all unmarried people masturbated instead of having intercourse. And at the same time, relief for unwed mothers could be kept to a minimum."

"Gosh! Is that how psychiatrists are born?"

"That's how this one was born. And it's been the basis for my whole theory of self-play. I prefer that term to self-abuse. It's a lot more accurate. Today I am probably the world's greatest authority on the subject. When my book comes out next month, I'll undoubtedly be swamped with calls to lecture to medical societies and civic groups. I'll see that you get a copy, autographed especially to Brick."

"Gee, Dr. Freund! I'll keep it in a place of honor in my library forever! Imagine! Me knowing a real author. Now I guess I better get going before Jack has the Marines out looking for me. But my ass end still hurts so much, I don't know how I'll ever pull my panties up over it!"

"Leave them here."

"But . . . what'll you do with them?"

"I don't know. Maybe I can use them for inspiration when I start my next book!"

Dr. Freund, as far as I was concerned, not only knew what he was talking about as a psychiatrist, but he also knew what he was talking about as a literary celebrity. His book hadn't been out three weeks, before he had so many bids to lecture on it to different social, medical, and economic groups, he had to eliminate half of his private practice just to keep all his dates. He even received a couple of honorary degrees from famous foundations as a result of his theories. Generally, doctors use only the M.D. degree on their stationery. But he was so pleased with one of his new ones that he had a special rubber stamp made. And from then on, when you got a bill in the mail from Dr. Freund, right after his medical degree, you found his new one, Doctor of Unilateral Sexuality, or D.U.S. At first, I didn't know what it meant. But he explained that it made him an Honorary Fellow of Masturbational Impulses, entitling him to take part in discussions at the Royal Academy in Addis Ababa.

Of course, some of the publicity he received wasn't exactly the friendly kind, like a pat on the back. It was a lot more like a kick in the pants. While one bunch would extol him as the greatest thing since contraception, another would hang him in effigy, label him the Antichrist, accuse him of being a corrupter of youth, and call for burning him at the stake. The Senate began to talk seriously about investigating him. Even Jack expressed a few doubts about my continuing as his patient. But I turned on the tears and won him over to my side without too much trouble. You would have thought that any idea that helped lower taxes would be received with delight. Of course, I had a sneaking suspicion that those who cheered him the loudest were the pussy-petters themselves, only too happy to find a scientific reason for having their fun without any danger. I don't think they gave a rap, one way or the other, about this wonderful method for the elimination of bastards from the world. All they wanted was a justification for going right on doing what they'd always done. Because now, even frustrated old maids and dirty old men could consider themselves as true benefactors of humanity. Those who wanted to hang him, of course, were the right-wing reactionaries, those eighteenth-century leftovers who never want to see change and progress made in any field.

Naturally, I was one of those Dr. Freund kept on as a patient. As a medical man, according to his oath, he couldn't desert me when I needed him so badly. And he liked to talk over any new ideas he developed with a sympathetic listener, which I certainly was. Besides, I had made him a solemn promise, when we'd played the horseback game, that I wouldn't do any more fucking until I was married. And he was such a conscientious little guy, he was determined to see I didn't break my word. I don't think he had too much faith in my strength of character. It wasn't that he didn't trust me. But he knew how susceptible I could be to certain suggestions. And I looked forward to my sessions with him with a great deal of happiness. While we talked about whatever was bothering me, or him, I could relax and pussy-pet to my heart's content, while he'd listen to my problems and once in a while suggest a different twist that allowed me to enjoy what I was doing even more. It wasn't the same as having his penis inside me, which is what I really wanted. But I was safeguarding my health, making sure I wouldn't get pregnant and add a further burden on the taxpayers of the city, and having myself a ball, all at the same time.

One day when I came into his office, he seemed

to be more excited than usual. And with Dr. Freund, that was something. At first sight, anyone who didn't know he was a psychiatrist would have thought he was an escaped lunatic. But I was used to him. And this day, he didn't seem able to stay seated while we were talking. He kept marching up and down in his office, sometimes moving so rapidly, if I hadn't known he was treating me, I'd have thought he was running a race with himself. He didn't like anyone prying into his private affairs, but after a few minutes, I just couldn't stand it anymore.

"Why are you so jittery?"

"Brick darling!" he shouted, excitement showing on his fat little face. "I've finally made it!"

"Made who?"

"Can't you think of anything but that?" he demanded angrily. "Does your so-called mind always have to make a beeline for what you've got between your legs?"

"That's my trouble. That's why Jack sent me to you in the first place . . . to get straightened out on pussy-petting and stuff. Don't tell me you've forgotten about the problem I had with Red Feather already?"

"Yes!" he shouted, throwing his arms wildly in the air. "I've forgotten about everything . . . even your fucking Indian!"

"Why?"

"Because this morning I received an invitation to address the Committee for a Sane Universe!"

"So?"

"Don't you know who they are?"

"A bunch of eggheads, I guess."

"Eggheads?" He stood still and just stared at me, shaking his head like an angry stallion. "If

58

I hadn't gotten myself so involved in your problems, I'd kick you the hell out of here this minute —right on your ass!"

"I'd rather you whipped it like when we played horsie," I giggled. "It was much more fun."

He fell back into his chair, giving me what I called his psychiatrist look. "Which was more fun . . . the whipping or the copulating?"

"I kind of liked them both," I muttered, wriggling in my chair at the memory. "But I have to admit the second act was a little more fun than the first."

"You know what you are?"

"What?"

"An oversexed, stupid, hot-pants little twot!"

"Isn't it awful!"

"Don't you ever set your mind on anything above the belt?"

"It never itches me up there. And you told me a thousand times not to waste your time with anything but facts."

"I don't know what I'm going to do with you," he sighed deeply. Then suddenly he banged his fist down on the desk top. "Yes I do!"

"What?"

"It might do you some good to see how a disciplined group studies masturbation . . . one interested only in pure scientific research."

"Gosh! Do you want to show me off to them as an example of something?"

"No! But I think it's time you began to realize how important these things can be to the future of mankind. How old are you?"

"Almost sixteen."

"Aren't you interested in making the world a better place for coming generations?"

59

"Of course!"

"Good! I'm going to give you a chance very few girls your age ever get."

"What's that?"

"I'm going to take you with me when I address the Committee," he announced grandly. "Do you think your guardian might object?"

"Why should he? You're my doctor, aren't you?"

"I am!"

"Then I'll just tell him you're trying a new kind of therapy," I giggled.

"What are you laughing at?"

"Are you also going to tell the Committee about your playing ring-around-the-flagpole?"

"What's that?"

"You know. The game you were playing the first time I came to your office . . . the one where you tried to throw ringers over that other man's pecker with doughnuts?"

Dr. Freund looked very insulted. "This is a scientific group," he said coldly. "They aren't interested in the nutty games a psychiatrist sometimes has to play with a disturbed patient. They are only interested in facts to help improve the world."

"Will your book do that?"

"They think so. And so do I."

Jumping up, I ran around the desk and fell into his lap. "I'll be so proud of you," I murmured, putting my arms around his neck and nibbling at his ear. "I really will!"

"Well . . . that's better," he finally muttered, sliding his hand up under my skirt until his hand rested on my pussy. "Have you been a good girl and kept your promise?"

"Oh, yes!"

"All right," he nodded, beginning to wiggle his fingers around inside me. "Just relax and the treatment will be all over in a couple of minutes."

I was thrilled right down to the marrow of my bones as I looked around the lecture hall of the University and saw how jam packed it was. Not only wasn't there a single empty seat in sight in the huge auditorium, but even the aisles at the back were crowded with standees, chattering away at each other and waiting with anticipation for Dr. Freund to begin his talk. Up to this moment, I had never realized how many people there were in the world who took such an active interest in pussy-petting. Because once you eliminated all the scientific gobbledygook, that's what masturbation was all about. And at the same time, I was delighted that out of all that throng, I was the only one who knew the speaker of the evening well enough to have seen him stark naked, to have had my bare bottom whipped by him, to have felt his erected pecker inside my pussy, and who was able to unburden my heart and soul to him every week, at twenty-five bucks a half-hour.

Seated in the rear, where Dr. Freund had insisted I remain so he wouldn't have to see my adoring expression every time he looked out over the audience, I wriggled about a little in my seat and began to take some notice of the people around me. All of them, men and women alike, seemed to be of the heavy intellectual type, with fancy educations, long academic degrees, and inquisitive interests far beyond my own. And staring at them, with their high-domed foreheads and their intense expressions, made me feel a tiny bit inadequate, in spite of everything else. Not one of the women looked as if they shaved under the arms, and other places, as carefully as I did. Nor did the aroma around me say very much for their use of deodorants. Just being intellectual seemed to make most of them careless about what no woman had a right to be careless about. Yet here I was, a girl who hadn't even finished high school, surrounded by some of the biggest and best scientific brains, of both sexes, in the city. It was enough to make me shiver, and feel almost as antsy-in-the-pants as if I were being locked in a room, naked, with a far-out group of folk singers, for a very private hootenanny.

Munching away steadily at the bag of caramels I had fortified myself with, I suddenly became aware of a hand pressing against my thigh, about half-way between my knee and my hip. Turning to stare at the occupant of the next seat, I saw a smallish young man, bearded and unkempt, wearing filthy blue jeans, a black turtle-neck sweater, a stained windbreaker, and badly scuffed thongs, leering happily in my direction. Aware of my inspection, he broadened his grin and removed his dirty-nailed fingers just as the lights in the auditorium dimmed, heralding the start of the program.

After an introduction that was so glowing I was hardly able to believe the chairman was talking about my medical confessor, the psychiatrist approached the podium to begin his lecture. Being a man who had little patience with the rules of propriety, he launched right into his topic of the evening—"Masturbational Practices Down Through the Ages, and Their Beneficial Effects Upon Human Society"—without so much as acknowledging the chairman's words. And as he began speaking, I slid far down into my seat to listen, chewing away on my caramels, and forgetting all about the strange-looking creature seated next to me.

But in the darkness, a moment or two later, I felt, once again, the exploring hand of my neighbor. This time, however, instead of being pressed gently against my leg on the outside of my skirt, it came out of nowhere to start a rapid climb up the inside of my thigh, underneath my clothing.

"Stop that!" I whispered fiercely, slapping at him with my bag of caramels.

In the quiet of the auditorium, my quick reaction and my loud whisper carried much further than I'd anticipated. Almost immediately, all sorts of hisses for silence echoed around me, startling me. And mixed in with them, I caught the definite sounds of amusement from the seat next to mine.

Angrily I defended myself against all of them with another loud whisper of protest. "How would you like it if he'd tried to grab your . . . pussy?"

But by this time, the audience was so caught up in what the doctor was saying, half of them didn't bother to shush me, while the rest made only a few half-hearted attempts. And I was forced to clutch at the young man's hand and yank it down and out from between my legs by main strength.

Leaning in his direction, I spoke again, as haughtily as I could. "Try that once more, you son of a bitch, and I'll clobber you!"

"Why?"

"That was my pussy you were putting your hand on!"

"Cool!"

"What do you think I am?"

"Real Sam!"

63

"Honest?"

"The whole bag. I'm hung up on red hair so don't bring me down, bird!"

"Why not?"

"Scientific curiosity."

"Ha!"

"This is a meeting of scientists, isn't it?"

"Yeah," I muttered. "That's why I can't understand what a creep like you is doing here."

"Trying to learn how anyone can take this masturbation jazz seriously," he whispered, grabbing my hand and shoving it in his lap to feel his erect pecker. "But this is how I dig you."

"Wow!"

"Like what do you say we do some research on our own?"

"How?"

"Like we go get a beer and compare organs."

Just the feel of his enormous pecker made me start to react exactly as I had that morning on the ranch, when Red Feather had walked into my cabin with my breakfast tray, finding me naked. Suddenly, the air in the auditorium became so stifling, I not only forgot all about my solemn promises to Dr. Freund, I forgot about Dr. Freund himself as well. I felt an irresistible impulse to move, even if it was only to stand on my feet.

"O.K.!" I whispered, getting up abruptly. "Let's go!"

Outside, in front of the building, I was a little surprised to discover I was several inches taller than my strange escort. But far from causing him any embarrassment, this physical disparity seemed to inflate his already extended ego. He strutted alongside of me like a rooster creating an impression in an alien barnyard, with his couched lance of knighthood standing out in front of him and stretching his jeans to the bursting point.

"Where are we going?" I asked.

"That depends."

"On what?"

"On how much bread you've got."

"How much I've got?" I repeated, coming to a dead stop. "I thought you asked me out for a beer!"

"I did," he murmured, easing me up against a building and pressing the front of his body against mine. "I'm taking you, too. All you've got to do is pay for it."

"Gosh!" I muttered, forcing my hand down between us to feel him again. "How can you walk around with that flagpole? It must reach all the way to your knees!"

"It's a real gasser!"

"Will it go away?"

"Yeah."

"How soon?"

"Right after work."

"You want to fuck me?"

"After a couple of beers."

"And you want me to pay for everything as well?"

"It's all in the interest of science," he grinned. "You are interested in science, aren't you?"

"Of course! But why do you talk so funny sometimes and not other times?"

"That's for the tourists. It goes with the threads I'm wearing."

"Well, before I go anywhere with you, I want to know your name?"

"Benjy."

"Benjy what?"

"Brodsky."

"Benjy, are you interested in pussy-petting?"

"Never saw any I want to pet."

"Then why did you go to the lecture?"

"I was bushed. All I wanted was a place to sit down. Then I saw you and got crotch-happy."

Once again I reached out to wrap my fingers around his swollen pigsticker. "Gee!" I muttered. "That's the biggest hunk of flagpole I ever felt."

"You feel many?"

"Will it last till we get to my house?"

"Hey!" he protested. "What about my beer?"

"There's lots in the fridge at home. Let's grab a cab right away."

"You paying?"

"Yes. I don't want anything to happen to you till we get there. I want to see more of you. From the size of that thing, you make Red Feather seem like a little boy!"

"Who's Red Feather?"

"Indian I once knew."

"Real red?"

"All over!"

"You can tell me about his action during the commercials."

"What commercials? We going on TV?"

"Don't put me on, chick. Even a siege gun like mine has to cool off between shots."

"I'm not so sure I want to tell you about Red Feather."

"It's in the interest of science. I'm writing a book."

"About what?"

"Fucking."

"Nobody writes a book about fucking."

"Nobody writes about anything else these days,"

he chuckled. "Academic freedom and all the free-speech movements have knocked down the barriers the reactionaries of the world have put up. I'm taking a doctorate at the University and the book is going to be my thesis."

"What's it called?"

" 'The Physiological and Psychological Effects of Regular Nightly Injections of Spanish Fly on the Female Reproductive System,' " he recited grandly.

"I never heard of anything so crazy."

"Of course it is. But these days you have to get a research grant and write a book if you want to get ahead in academic circles. And when I get to be a professor at Vassar, I'll be able to test every one of my theories on my students."

"Do you think they'll like your system of teaching?"

"I don't know. But I will!"

Taking Benjy home for a couple of beers caused a bigger change in my life than anything since the day I was born. It didn't start out to be that way, because at the time I had no intention of changing my way of living. I was having too much fun the way things were going to take a chance on ruining everything. After all, it wasn't every girl of fifteen who had the freedom I had. My parents were dead, Wong How was learning to be a little afraid of me, and Jack, my guardian, whom I loved so desperately, was such a rock-head he couldn't recognize the real thing when he came face to face with it. About all I can say for him is that he didn't interfere with me very much. There probably wasn't another girl in the whole world who wouldn't have peed in her pants in church just to switch places with me.

As Dr. Freund used to say, it would be a better world if the subconscious desire to reproduce could be subordinated to the human desire for pleasure with safety. To his way of thinking, this was pussy-petting. Not that fucking wasn't a pleasure as well. And being the product of a progressive upbringing, I was completely dedicated to my own pleasure. But there were a few pitfalls with the real thing that didn't exist with the hand-jobs, such as getting pregnant or coming down with a dose of the clap. But I guess I had too great a yen for the real thing to be satisfied indefinitely with a kid's game. Incidently, from the moment I felt Benjy's hand on my pussy in the University lecture hall, I never saw Dr. Freund again. It wasn't that I didn't need him any longer. At times, all of us need someone to listen to our troubles. I just would have felt a little silly trying to defend my liking for reaching a climax in the old-fashioned way with a character who believed most of the world's problems could be solved if every person got on a more intimate basis with his or her own genitals.

When we got to the house, I took Benjy straight into the living room and left him sprawled out on the couch, while I hurried into the kitchen for the beer. At the time, I thought how lucky I was Jack wasn't home. Because if there was one thing he couldn't stand, it was to see a man or a woman lounging on the furniture with no respect for it. I suppose no one outgrows every one of their silly ideas. And if Benjy ever had any respect for anything besides himself, I never found out what it was. It didn't help matters either that he turned

68

out to be a sloppy drinker, refusing to use a glass and managing to spill half the beer, not only on himself and the couch, but on me as well, his having insisted on my sharing the cushions with him so he could put his hand up under my skirt while we talked.

I don't remember just where, but I once read on one of my periodic searches for knowledge that drinking men have little interest in women, as long as the brew holds out. I never really believed it, but it certainly proved to be true with Benjy. As soon as he got comfortable on the couch, with an open beer can in his hand, that hunk of flagpole between his legs became as meek as a kitten. It softened up so quickly I got scared. But he kept insisting he could put it through its paces any time he felt like. Though he didn't seem in too much of a hurry to give me a demonstration. He was very impressed with the apartment and the furnishings. He kept looking around the living room like he'd never seen furniture and rugs before. I was dying to know where he lived, but he seemed so happy in my house, I didn't have the nerve to ask. And when I showed him where the bathroom was, just in case the beer ran through his kidneys a little quickly, he let out such a howl I was afraid he'd disturb the neighbors. He wanted to try everything at once, just to make sure it all worked. And since Jack, in spite of my progressive upbringing, had taught me that a hostess' duty was to make her guests feel at home, I let him do anything he wanted. He called it the fanciest damn shithouse he'd ever seen. But when he wanted me to demonstrate how the bidet worked (it was my bathroom and Jack was a complete nut on physical cleanliness), I figured things had gone far enough, and I insisted we go back to the living room for more beer.

It must have been my lucky night, because I was in the kitchen opening another batch of cans when Jack came home. Hearing him in the living room, I blew a quick kiss to my good fairy. Because I know I never would have been able to explain what Benjy's hand was doing under my skirt. Particularly after Jack had spent so much money sending me to Dr. Freund's every week, just to be cured of that weakness. But when I came in, carrying the open cans on a tray, I wasn't really too surprised to find Jack standing in front of the couch, staring down at Benjy as if he were an animal in the zoo. Even though I already loved him dearly, I have to admit Benjy wasn't the type to make the best first impression on anybody.

Seeing me, Jack gave a loud sigh of relief. "Brick?" he asked, gesturing toward the couch. "Where in God's name did you find that? And what is it?"

Putting down the tray, I turned on my most brilliant smile. "Jack, I'd like you to meet Benjy Brodsky. Benjy, this is my guardian, Jackson Brant."

Having already told me he considered good manners an outmoded concept, Benjy didn't bother to get up. "Hi!" he said, waving his hand at Jack.

"Hi!" muttered Jack, falling into a chair.

"I met Benjy at the lecture," I explained, sitting down next to my guest.

"Oh? I thought it was for intellectuals only."

"Benjy's very intelligent," I protested quickly. "He's even studying at the University."

"To be what?"

"A Ph.D. in humanities," Benjy answered, sitting up with a jerk that spilled beer down the front of his clothes and almost bumped me off the couch onto the floor.

Jack seemed surprised. "That means you must have already graduated from college and taken your Master's as well."

"Right!"

My guardian stared at Benjy curiously. "I don't mean to be nosy, but where did you get the money for so much schooling?"

"In our enlightened society only slobs pay for education."

"Then how . . . ?"

"The government!"

"I see. That sort of makes me one of your slobs . . . as a taxpayer, I mean."

"That it does," Benjy nodded complacently. "But you can afford it and I can't. I went to a public high school, to college on the G.I. Bill, and got my Master's the same way. It didn't cost me a cent."

"Isn't he wonderful?" I gushed at Jack. "Benjy's told me he's going to be a professor at Vassar someday."

But ignoring me completely, Jack kept his eyes on Benjy. "How long did you serve in the Army?"

"About three and a half months."

"Pretty short hitch, wasn't it?"

"They didn't think so. They discharged me for being a disturbing influence on morale."

"I can't imagine why," Jack muttered half to himself. "Who's paying the bills for you now? You working?"

"You're putting me on."

"Who then?"

71

"Some stupid married broad."

"How come?"

"Blackmail."

"What?"

"Don't get turned on," Benjy shrugged. "It's kid stuff. I got into her pants a few times, and she went for me so big, she kept begging for more. That's when I lowered the boom. I told her I'd tip off her old man to what she was doing when he was at his office unless she came through with enough for two years at the University."

"And she agreed . . . just like that?"

"Soon as she saw the pictures."

"What pictures?"

"The ones I had a pal of mine take when I was in the bag with her. And she had some real crazy ideas about screwing too. Some of the shots were so far out, I was able to sell them to a guy specializing in pornography."

"Pretty lousy for her, wasn't it?"

"Just paying her dues."

"What do you expect to do after finishing school?"

"Probably join up with the Peace Corps for a while," answered Benjy, stretching lazily. "Just for background. Then I think I'll take a whack at teaching."

"You got the integrity for either?"

"Who needs it? Teaching is a breeze. And the Peace Corps is just a chance to see the world on the taxpayers."

"The Navy used to use that as a slogan."

"For suckers!"

"And you're no sucker."

"Right!"

"Jack!" I exploded excitedly. "Can't you just see

72

Benjy at some big reception, in striped trousers and a cutaway, talking to a king or a queen?"

"No."

"Why?"

"Because I don't think they're hard up enough yet to let bums like him attend their receptions."

Benjy jumped to his feet quickly. "I might have known," he said nastily. "From your high and mighty seat on Easy Street, it doesn't take much for your kind to sneer at my kind."

"That isn't true!" Jack protested loudly.

"Why not, cube?"

"Because if it weren't for my kind, there wouldn't be any of your kind."

"Why is that?"

"We've coddled you, protected you, and made everything easy for you," said Jack angrily. "We've gone miles out on a limb excusing you when we should have cracked down hard on you. If it weren't for people like me, you'd have had to go to work years ago instead of living on the tax-payers and blackmailing silly women!"

"That's a crock of shit!"

Being a very liberal-minded man, and having lived with me as long as he had, language usually didn't bother Jack very much. But for some reason, Benjy's saying "shit" made him blow his top. I couldn't understand why, because I said it myself all the time. But I suppose he just didn't like Benjy, or recognize any of his good qualities the way I did. Anyway, he jumped to his feet in a rage.

"Get out!" Jack yelled, pointing toward the door. "Get out, you filthy little bum!"

"Jack!" I jumped up myself. "That's no way to talk to my guest!"

"I'll talk any damn way I want!" he shouted angrily. "If I ever catch you with this . . . gutter rat again, I'll make you good and sorry. I ought to have my brains examined for letting you go to that idiotic lecture with a nut like Freund."

"Oh?" said Benjy with a smile. "Then you think all that jazz about saving the world through masturbation is for the birds?"

"I certainly do!"

"Me too! I've always found fucking to be much more satisfying!"

"Brick!" Jack screamed. "Brick! Go to your room this instant!"

And the last sight I had of poor Benjy that night was his struggling and kicking as Jack picked him up bodily and carried him in the direction of the front door.

The mattress was lumpy, the blanket itchy, and the room ice cold. I pressed myself as closely as I could against Benjy's skinny backside, even wrapping my legs around his, taking care not to injure that incredible flagpole he carried around with him. The snores of the other sleepers sounded awfully loud in the darkness, and I was uncomfortably aware how different this place was from my lovely room at home. But I supposed I shouldn't think of Jack's apartment as home anymore. I had made the break myself, as cleanly as I could. From now on, wherever Benjy was would be home to me, even though we were being forced, because of certain financial difficulties, to share it with two other couples.

Strangely, I wasn't the least bit embarrassed when Benjy would push his enormous pecker into me with other people in the room. My having been raised to consider all physical functions as natural probably had something to do with it. As a matter of fact, instead of feeling self-conscious, I enjoyed it. And Benjy being the greedy little character he was, I was able to enjoy myself several times a night. I liked their knowing we were fucking. And I hoped our panting, our groaning, and our creaking bedsprings bothered them as much as theirs sometimes bothered me. I guess what I really minded was being a spectator. I had always been such an active girl, I only felt at ease when I was actually participating.

The room we lived in was furnished with a rickety set of double-deck bunks and a single bed. Benjy and I drew the lower in the double-decker. Right above us, Ginger and Ernest only fucked three times a week. Ernest, being in training to become a professional fighter, didn't want to use up his strength unnecessarily. This didn't seem to bother him when he beat Ginger up, which he'd already done several times, but he was convinced that coming more than three times a week would sap the vital reserve he needed for his ring work. But across the room, Molly and Jacob made so much racket in their single bed when they were banging away, I was scared it would collapse on top of them, and we'd all have to sleep in shifts. But, luckily, it never did.

In order to keep everything up to date, I ought to explain how I came to be here, in this one-room cold-water pigsty in Hoboken. It was a long way from the University, but Benjy decided the cheap rent more than made up for any inconvenience. There wasn't even a bathroom in the place, which made me understand, for the first time, why Benjy went so far off his rocker the night I had shown him mine. The toilet, when it worked, was down at the end of the hall. And though all of us, except Ginger, who never wore any and was naked, stood around in our underwear, washing in the cold water in our sink, if we wanted to take care of anything more urgent, we had to go out into that drafty hallway. So I always kept putting it off till the last possible minute. The only trouble was that everyone else on our floor did the same thing, and it made for some pretty heavy traffic jams and a lot of frantic banging on the door once in a while. Being as unself-conscious as I was, I wouldn't have minded if the thing had been a two-seater, but everyone else protected their privacy by locking themselves in.

Anyway, several days after Jack had tossed Benjy out of the apartment—days in which he and Wong How chewed me out about my lack of class consciousness every chance they got—I happened to come face to face with my beatnik Casanova during an outing one afternoon. He was as taken with me as I was with him, and he'd been hanging around the neighborhood, hoping for a chance to talk to me. But I think I took him by surprise, because when I saw him, I threw myself into his arms and began kissing him like crazy, exactly the way I'd always wanted Jack to kiss me. But he was so busy being a playboy with every glamour girl in town, while acting the stern guardian with me, I just got terribly discouraged about his ever getting a yen in my direction. And I'd made up my mind to take off with Benjy if he'd have me. A girl needs to be wanted by somebody, even if he is only a second-rate beatnik. It's an important part of the female's psychological makeup. Benjy wasn't much to look at, he didn't have a dime, and I found out he'd hit me good and hard if I dared to disagree with him. But he was male, he did have that gorgeous flagpole dangling down to his knees, he was full of plans for remaking the world into what he thought it ought to be, and when he remembered, he said he loved me. Which was an awful lot more than Jack ever had said.

So without even going back into the house for my toothbrush, Benjy and I took off for Hoboken, where he said he had his pad with two other couples. My coming with him would make everything perfect. Now each of the men would have his own girl, making it unnecessary for Benjy to have to get along with the others' leavings. They could even do a little pussy-swapping if things became dull. I was a little surprised to find everybody living and eating and even washing in the same room, but I was so happy over finding Benjy again, and so determined to show Jack I could take care of myself and get along without him, I was willing to make the best of anything. I moved into that lower bunk with my lover, I was given a rusty hook for my clothes, there being no closet of any kind, and I was ready to stand up and fight the world for my way of life.

In the beginning, I admit I was a little leery about taking off my clothes and going to bed in a room full of strange people. It wasn't that I didn't want Benjy to fuck me, which I knew he would do right away because of the way his flagpole was reacting, but I wasn't sure I wanted him to do it in front of the others. But that first night every bit of my uneasiness, which shouldn't have existed anyway, because if there is one thing a progressive education teaches a person it is to be free, easy, and forward-looking about everything, was wiped away like chalk marks being erased from a blackboard with a wet rag. The others must have been a little uncertain themselves, because they sat around watching me to see what I would do. But I just lay down with my clothes on and did nothing, determined not to move until they did. After a while, I guess they got tired. And before I could even blink an eye, first Ginger and Ernest, and then Molly and Jacob, casually took off all their clothes in front of me, and walked around naked for a while before climbing into bed. Looking at the other guys, I laughed a little to myself. Next to Benjy, they were built like little boys, or, at least, what I thought little boys were built like. And I got a kick out of the way the other girls sneaked looks at my boy, when he got around to taking his pants off. He may have been built like a little boy, in every place but one. There, he was one hundred percent king-size.

But this night, along with being cold, I was a little unhappy, and my face still stung where Benjy had slapped me a short time before. I didn't really mind his hitting me because there was a lot to be said for his viewpoint. I wouldn't even have cared too much if he'd have forced me to climb into bed with one of the other men, particularly Ernest, who looked like he knew everything there was to know about giving a girl a first-class fucking. But what I did mind was that our quarrel had four very nosy spectators, each of them hanging on everything we said, and several times offering words of advice to one or the other of us.

It seems the men were having difficulty getting

78

together the next month's rent on the apartment, if one room with no heat, no closet, and rusty-running cold water could be called an apartment. Ernest's manager, a greasy little pimp with a chewed-up cigar butt always in his mouth, wouldn't get him a fight. He kept saying Ernest wasn't ready yet, but I don't think he knew how to arrange a match. I guess he preferred to let his tiger go on relief. Jacob was a beatnik, like Benjy. But also, he was a poet and a half-assed folk singer. He spent all his time just sitting around, strumming on his goddamn guitar, and composing poems that were so bad I couldn't blame the editors who threw him out when he showed up at their offices with a new batch, every month or so. Benjy, of course, was a student at the University. And all the money he'd blackmailed from that married woman for his education was gone. Like myself, the two women were good for nothing. I, at least, had the excuse of having spent my formative years in some fancy schools, run by very fancy progressive educators, being prepared for illiteracy. Ginger and Molly, on the other hand, coming as they did from slum backgrounds, should have been able to do something to bring in a little money. The desire of a person to improve and climb out of the slums is supposed to be very strong, at least according to everyone who writes about these unfortunates. But maybe they don't know as much as they think they do, a fault with a great many intellectuals, because the only desire these dames had was to fuck, and make the most nauseating meals I ever tasted. I learned not to say anything to them about their cooking, because when I mentioned it the first time I'd eaten one of their dinners, they got very insulted.

Both of them told me that if I didn't like their cooking, I could take over the job myself, or go fuck a duck. So I decided to mind my own business.

All this, added to the lack of money, didn't make for a happy atmosphere in our crowded dormitory. And tonight, when Benjy finally suggested I ask Jack for money, I got on my high horse and told him to drop dead.

"You stupid little fluff!" said Ginger, hanging over the edge of the upper bunk until her head was almost in my face. "You gotta!"

"I gotta what?"

"Ask your rich daddy for dough. Ain't you got pride? You want us all to wind up in the bread line?"

"He's not my daddy, and I wouldn't care if you wound up in the shithouse!"

"He ain't your daddy?"

"No," I mimicked her surprised tone of voice. "He ain't my daddy!"

"Then what is he, for Christ's sake?"

"My guardian."

"You mean an old fart who likes to take care of a little girl so he can play with her pussy?"

"No, you dumb stupid twot!" I shouted angrily. "He's a fine gentleman! But I think there's another way I might be able to get some money."

"How?"

I looked around at the others before answering. "Well," I said tentatively, "I could always go on . . . the stage!"

"Aw . . . what can you do?" Benjy laughed sarcastically.

"I can sing and I can dance. And you told me

yourself I can make love better than anyone you ever knew."

"I'll stick up for that," laughed Ernest. "Any broad that can handle the hunk of meat that little bastard carries around has got to know what she's doing."

"Mind your own fucking business!" Benjy yelled up at Ernest.

"Careful, Ernest," Molly giggled from across the room. "You're liable to make Battling Benjy mad."

"Fuck you too!" hollered my lover.

"I wouldn't mind it a bit," laughed Molly. Then she pushed at Jacob insistently. "Jacob, are you going to let that little squirt talk to me that way?"

"Lemme alone!" Jacob growled angrily.

"Why?"

"I'm working on a poem, you stupid son of a bitch!"

"What's it about?" asked Ginger curiously.

"A crock of shit, I'll bet," Benjy muttered.

"Shut up, you . . . you beatnik!" screamed Jacob in a rage.

I couldn't help it. I started to giggle, and Benjy's hand suddenly cracked across my face, making my head ring like a bell. "That goes for you too!" he ordered angrily. "I'll tell you when to talk!"

"Dig the new Hitler!" jeered Ernest. "Isn't he the creep who's always hollering about free speech? I guess he means it only for himself. I never thought there was a girl around he could lick!"

"You leave Benjy alone, you big bastard!" I sobbed, tears starting to trickle down my face. "He can lick me any time he wants to!"

Benjy grabbed my arm roughly. "You going to ask your old man for dough?"

81

"No!"

Crack! His hand smacked across the other side of my face, making me cry as hard as I could, with enough noise to wake up the whole building.

"Give it to her good!" Ginger urged fiercely, leaning so far out of her bunk to watch what was happening that she started to fall out until Ernest grabbed her and yanked her back.

"With a strap!" Molly shouted encouragingly from the other side of the room. "Across her bare ass! She's only a kid. She needs a good lesson in respect!"

Suddenly Jacob stood up in his bed, stepping all over Molly in the process. "Quiet, goddamn it!" he shouted at the top of his lungs. "How can I get any work done with you bastards making all that racket?"

"You work?" Ginger asked scornfully.

"I am a poet!"

"Poet . . . shit!" she screamed gleefully. "You're a bum!"

With all this bedlam around me, I crouched down beside Benjy, holding onto him with both arms, and crying as if I'd never be able to stop. We belonged to each other, and if he wanted to hit me, even with a strap, it was nobody else's business. But the idea of his doing it in front of these terrible people, and even paying some attention to their suggestions, was just too much for a sensitive young girl like me. I was used to being coddled and pampered. I shouldn't have had to face any of the ugliness of life in the raw. Nobody had ever told me things could be like this. I hid my head in the dirty pillow and howled until they all started screaming at me to shut up. Finally, after all the neighbors began banging on

82

the walls, the floors, and the ceilings, things quieted down enough for the rest of them, including Benjy, to fall asleep, leaving me to huddle against him, still a little teary, worrying about how we would get the money for the rent, and wondering what Jack would say if he could see me now, beaten, cold, hungry, and lonely.

Some weeks later, when I was alone in the room late one afternoon, Benjy came sneaking in looking as guilty as a school chaplain caught in a car in Lovers' Lane with a naked coed. Ernest was over at the gym working out, and Ginger was watching. Molly was at work. And God alone knew where Jacob was. He was such a nut, he could have hopped a freight for California if he'd been working on a sonnet about the sunset and wanted to take a look at one as far West as he could get.

I greeted my proud rebel curiously. "What's the idea of sneaking in here like a lousy fink?"

"You're in trouble," he mumbled.

"Why?"

He came over and slumped down next to me on our bunk. "The others have decided to try you."

"Try me for what?"

"Fucking around."

"That isn't true!" I exploded. "I've never let anyone touch me but you. Not even Ernest, though he shows me his pigsticker all the time, hoping to slide it in my pants."

"That's not the kind of fucking they mean."

"What other kind is there?"

"Like sitting around on your ass all day and

83

refusing to do anything to help . . . like getting a job maybe, and bringing in a little money."

"How much do you bring in?"

"I am a student!"

"So?"

"So there was a meeting yesterday and Molly insisted you had to be tried," muttered my hero, a hangdog expression on his homely face. "Not that you'll be able to do anything. She's already decided you're guilty. And you know what that means."

Maybe if I had known what was going to happen when I refused to do a simple thing like ask Jack for money for our rent, I might have had a few second thoughts about it. But I'm not really sure, because I've always been blessed with a happy-go-lucky disposition. No matter what catastrophe stared me in the face, I was always sure something good was bound to turn up to take care of everything. Jack used to tell me, even when I was pretty small, that I must be a changeling, a reincarnation of some character named Micawber. Who he was I haven't the faintest idea. But my guardian was such a great one for kidding and having a few laughs, I've always been half convinced anyone with a name like that had to be made up right out of his own mind.

But what actually happened proved that you never can judge a person by appearances. Our landlord was the kind of monster who wouldn't hesitate to toss us all out into the street, even in the middle of a blizzard. And certainly, Benjy and those two other characters who lived with us weren't exactly the most stable of people. Ginger and Molly I disregarded completely, which only goes to show how wrong a person can be. The three of us broads never got along too well, except on the surface. I suppose it was because I considered them to be nothing but dirty-assed trollops, and they looked on me as a fresh young snot with too much pussy-itch. Benjy was a student and busy most of the time with his thesis. Ernest was in training, and couldn't do very much about our situation until his manager got lucky and found him a few fights. Or maybe Ernest was lucky he couldn't. Jacob, of course, was a poet and worth absolutely nothing to anyone, not even himself. So you can imagine my shock when the first thing Molly did, after learning of our predicament, was to go out and get herself a job as a waitress in a hash joint. She even talked poor Jacob into hiring on as a dishwasher in the same beanery. But after the first hour, the poor dope had busted so many dishes, the boss kicked him right out into the alley and told him not to come back, even as a customer. The only thing Ginger was good for was to hustle on the streets. And she was more than willing, but she knew that Ernest would have kicked the bejesus out of her if she did. So that let her out.

I, of course, made no attempt to do anything. With my background, I didn't feel it was up to me to help support anyone. I may have been raised to have a strong social conscience, but it wasn't strong enough to make me lift a finger to help these slobs. I was perfectly contented to go on fucking Benjy every night, and trusting to God that I got enough to eat during the day. That left it strictly up to Molly, who became the only breadwinner of the group. And with the very first paycheck she brought home, our little love nest turned into the worst kind of a matriarchy. You'd have thought she invented money. Molly was the boss, and ordered the rest of us around like slaves. And since she was the only one who brought home any groceries, we all did as we were told. She put us over the jumps every chance she got, but she saved the worst of her spite for me. I was the youngest, and I was the prettiest by far. But what was even worse to Molly, now that she'd become a steady wage earner and a capitalist, was that I refused to work.

No matter where I wind up someday in my travels, there's one thing I'll always be able to say for my life in Hoboken with this bunch of beatniks. It may have been rough in places, and there may have been times I was cold and hungry, but no one could ever describe it as dull. I used to wonder sometimes, when I was by myself in that awful room, whether Jack ever made any attempts to find me and rescue me from what he'd have called a fate worse than death. Because in spite of his belief in the progressive philosophy, and his quickness to promote the new rather than defend the old, he could be a pretty rigid character about a few things. And heading the list was his reverence for virginity in young girls, particularly mine. When I used to point out that he didn't seem to feel the same way toward those glamour pusses he ran around with, he'd get very red and gruff, and tell me to remember he was my guardian, and I had to do what he told me. This inability, on his part, to appreciate my point of view, is about the only thing I can say against him. Otherwise, he was a complete doll, and the only man I ever really loved. But when a number of weeks passed without his finding me, I came to the unhappy conclusion he'd decided to write me off and let me make my own way.

I'd better explain right here that when our little oasis of free expression and rebellion against society had become a matriarchy, Molly had drawn up and ratified a kind of constitution for us, with herself as president and dictator. Immediately, the right of any one of us to disagree with her became nonexistent. If anyone dared to argue, or didn't do as they were ordered, they were to be given a regular trial, with herself as prosecutor, judge, and jury. And her personal penal code contained only two sentences, outright expulsion, which was never handed down because that would have decreased her subjects, or whipping, administered by her, of course.

Right now, I stared at Benjy with frightened eyes. "You mean she'd really wh-whip m-me? Really?"

"Till your ass looks like two hunks of raw liver. Molly doesn't like you very much."

I stared at my courageous, loud-mouthed rebel against authority, forcing him to look back at me. "Did you defend me against her?"

Immediately, all the glamour that had once attached itself to Benjy, in my eyes, oozed off the little bastard as he weaseled and stammered, trying to justify his failure to take my part.

"You didn't!" I accused him.

"I'm tipping you off, am I not?"

"Sure," I said, disgusted by his open treachery. "Sure, you're tipping me off all right . . . to just what a yellow-bellied little rat-fink you are!"

Jumping off the bunk, I started gathering up my few possessions, like toothbrush and comb and stuff, while Benjy slumped on the edge and watched me. After a while, what I was doing seemed to sink into the rat's consciousness, and he got to his feet quickly.

"What do you think you're doing?" he demanded.

"Getting out!"

"Why?"

"If you think I'm going to hang around this shithouse so Molly, the bitch, can get her kicks walloping my ass end, you're really off your rocker!"

He came and grabbed my arm. "Please, chick?" he begged. "Why don't you stay? It won't be too bad. She promised!"

"That does it!" I yelled in a fury. "So you voted guilty too!"

"You know Molly," he muttered. "When that one gets an idea into her head, nothing can get it out short of dynamite."

He tried to take me into his arms, pushing me, during the process, with his hips so I could feel the awakening of his flagpole. But I was young and strong and mad. And I pushed back so hard, he went flying across the room.

"After all," he whined, crawling back toward me. "She does supply us with food, and she does pay the rent. We owe her something."

"Not the skin I sit on, you son of a bitch! Let her blister yours!"

"What about us?"

"What about us?"

"Don't you feel anything?"

Suddenly the very sight of the little rat, together with the dirt and filth of the room, got to be more than I could stomach. I wrenched open the door and turned around to face him, unable to leave without delivering the curtain oration the actress inside of me demanded.

"After several months of feeling you," I said coldly, projecting my voice as dramatically as if I were Camille in person, bidding her lover farewell, "I realize you're only a rotten little fart with hair. You make noise like you're a big-time rebel against society, but the minute your own comfort is involved, you become as gutless as a rabbit. The only thing you've got going for you is that oversized hunk of gristle hanging between your legs. If it hadn't been for that, I don't think I'd have pissed on any part of you!"

Turning and slamming the door behind me, I ran from that firetrap of a building, with everything I owned in my pockets, and started walking, without any idea where I was going, or what I'd do when I got there.

It seemed as if I'd been walking for days. I knew, of course, that I hadn't, but my poor feet sure felt as if I had. "Piss, shit, and corruption!" as Ginger was always saying, I was beat, used up, and pooped out. Running away from home, the way I had with Benjy, without taking anything with me but the clothes on my back, my shoes were worn pretty thin. And that was putting it mildly. But while I'd been living in that cozy little love nest my bearded beatnik had taken me to, he never had any money to give me to buy others, or have my old ones repaired. Sometimes, I wonder if he would have given me any even if he'd had some. One thing life was teaching me, to my great disappointment, more and more each day. And that was that no matter how much noise a person makes about social rebellion, and improving the lot of unfortunates enough to help them toward a secure future in freedom, this kind of humanitarian crusade is always carried on with somebody else's cash. Never a single penny belonging to the character doing the hollering is ever used. As a matter of fact, the louder the phony-baloney yells, the less chance there is to hit him for the loan of anything. And everything Benjy, that little rat-fink, did, he did with as much noise as possible.

Naturally, in my present state, I hadn't been paying any attention to where I was going, or to anything else around me. I wasn't even sure of my direction. I simply kept on walking the way I'd been facing when I ran out of that awful tenement in Hoboken. So I hadn't been particularly aware that numbers of airplanes were flying low over my head, coming and going in all directions. I can't even remember hearing them. Maybe the fact that it was pitch-black night by now had something to do with it. All I do know for sure is that just when I was sure I was going to pass out from exhaustion, I noticed I was right across the highway from Newark Airport. Just seeing it picked me up a little, and I headed straight for the field with a new burst of energy.

From the time I'd been a dirty-pants little kid, I'd always had a thing about airplanes and flying. Once in a while, during school vacations, when Jack would take me somewhere by air, or let me fly by myself, it felt like I was in seventh heaven. So now, instead of heading for the administration building, there being no point to that because I didn't have a cent in my pockets and everything in such a place has a price tag on it, I walked toward a large hangar, in front of which several commercial passenger planes were parked. I was so tired I didn't even notice the name painted all over the building. I was just drawn toward it like steel filings toward a magnet, feeling confident that if I could reach one of those planes, I'd be as safe as if I were home in bed once again in Jack's apartment. Call it a childish hallucination, or anything else you like, but I was an awfully weary, very hungry, and completely disillusioned nearly-sixteen-year-old girl, and all I wanted was to climb into one of those big four-engined friendly-looking birds and go to sleep.

The cabin door of one of them was wide open, and one of those portable stairways they use at airports was pushed right up against it. To me, it seemed like fate finally was starting to smile on me after a long succession of ugly frowns. But I'd no sooner placed one foot carefully on the first step than I was grabbed from behind by a pair of the strongest hands I'd ever felt. Twisting about as well as I could, I found myself staring up into the eyes of a husky gray-haired man, dressed in a pair of mechanic's coveralls. Immediately, he dragged me back to the ground.

"Where do you think you're going, Miss?" he asked in a sort of growl.

"I just wanted to peek inside," I said, nodding toward the plane and smiling as cheerfully as I could. I figured I was shabby enough looking so he wouldn't suspect I'd ever been on a passenger airliner before.

"You're old enough to know that ain't allowed," he muttered. "Fact is, you shouldn't even be on the field. You belong in the administration building. Maybe I oughta take you into the back of the hangar and work your backside over some with a piece of board."

One of the accomplishments I'd always prided myself on, and the one I was sure indicated a career on the stage for me if I ever wanted one, was my ability to cry at will. I could tell from a look at this man's expression that he wasn't kidding one bit. A wrong word from me now and I'd wind up with the blistered bottom Molly wanted to give me. Quickly I squeezed a couple of tears from the corners of my eyes and sobbed softly. "N-not that! P-please! That's what I've just run away from!"

"Folks been beating you?"

"N-not my f-family," I quavered. "The p-p-people I live w-with."

"You an orphan?"

"Y-y-yes."

Holding my arm tightly, he pulled me over to the front of the hangar, where the light was a lot stronger, and he could get a better look at me. "Beat you a lot, do they?"

"All the time! It's awful! That's why I ran away. I couldn't stand it anymore."

"Come far?"

"Miles and miles!"

"You do look kinda used up," he murmured slowly in a much more sympathetic tone, eying me up and down closely. "Hungry?"

"Oh, yes!"

"I'll make you a deal," he smiled, suddenly looking a lot younger and a whole lot nicer. "You sit down on that chair over there and stay put, and I'll get you a couple of hamburgers. I know what it's like to be hungry."

"I promise!" I clutched at him quickly, the very

92

thought of food making my mouth water bucket-fuls. "I promise!"

"Take cream in your coffee?"

"No. I like it black and strong."

"Smart kid," he nodded, starting me toward the chair with a friendly slap on the behind. "Be back in a couple of minutes."

About a half-hour later, I leaned back in my chair, comfortable once more and smiling at my newfound friend. No longer did he look either menacing or forbidding. And when he smiled back, I was sure he meant it exactly as a kind and considerate parent smiling at a loving daughter. Trying as hard as I could to keep from yawning, I noticed, out of the corner of my eye, that the portable stairway was still in place against the side of the plane with the open door. And while I was wondering how I was going to get into that ship without his seeing me, the phone started ringing in the office down at the far end of the huge hangar. Once again, it seemed, for the second time in less than an hour, the Good Fairy was smiling in my direction.

"Back in a couple of minutes," he called over his shoulder as he hurried down toward the other end of the building.

"I'll be here waiting," I called after him.

I wasn't particularly proud of what I was about to do, more so because it was to a nice guy like Don. While I'd been eating, he'd already told me his name was Don Preston, and he was the mechanic in charge of this hangar for Overseas Charter Service. But the first law of nature is self-preservation, and I intended to obey this law, even if it meant hurting my benefactor. Actually, I couldn't see that I'd be doing him any great

93

amount of harm anyway. I had just made up my mind that I was going to take a good long nap in that plane, and hell or high water wasn't going to stop me. As soon as Don had disappeared around the corner into the office, I made a beeline for the stairs leading up into the ship. I ran through the passenger section without stopping, and down a couple of steps into a private sort of compartment, just behind and below the pilot's cabin. There was a soft heavy mat of some kind in there. I couldn't tell exactly what it was because there were no lights on in the plane, and I wasn't equipped with matches. But wrapping myself in it, I stretched out and made myself as comfortable as possible. There seemed to be plenty of room. In a minute or two, I heard Don come back, calling my name. Another mechanic must have come along about then, because I heard him ask someone: "You seen a girl, about sixteen, or so, with red hair, around here anywhere?"

"I ain't seen a soul, Don," a man's voice answered.

"I told the little bugger to wait." Don sounded disappointed. "But I guess she got scared and ran off."

"That's the trouble with kids today," the other voice grunted in a disagreeable tone. "Never want to do what they're told. Need their tails walloped regular. But these days it's against the law to lay a finger on 'em!"

Then I heard Don start to chuckle softly. "I don't think you'd want to wallop this kid's tail."

"Why? She special or somethin?"

"A regular little doll, even beat up the way she was. Soon as a feller'd get her pants down, five would get you ten he'd start growing some different ideas."

With this compliment ringing in my ears, I fell asleep almost immediately. And while I have no way of knowing, I'm sure my lips must have been smiling over the last thing I ever heard Don say.

I don't know how long I slept, but from the way I fell off into dreamland, I figure I could teach psychiatrists like Dr. Freund a thing or two about handling wealthy patients who complain of a sleeping problem. For some reason, this disease never seems to attack the poor. I used to get tickled pink, during my regular weekly visits to his office, by the hordes of mink-coated, fat-assed dowagers who came running to him for help, without a darn thing wrong with any of them. They'd moan and they'd groan about the endless nights they spent walking the floors, their reactions to sleeping pills, and even the number of belts they were forced to take when the barbiturates wouldn't do the job by themselves. But in all that weeping and wailing, one important factor was never mentioned. In order for a person to sleep properly, he or she has to become tired. And believe me, I have a sure cure for all of them. Just start them out in Hoboken, and make them walk, nonstop, to the Newark Airport. They'd sleep all right. And if they didn't, they'd die, either of which result wouldn't have too much effect on the future of the world.

Some time later—it must have been several hours after I'd corked off as near as I can figure from what happened afterward—my sleep was disturbed by a lot of heavy objects being piled all over me. But I was so groggy, all I can remember is trying to push back at them for a couple of minutes until I was able to work myself into a comfortable position against them. And as soon as I did, I must have gone off again. Because I'll never forget how surprised I was when I finally did wake up to find myself stiff with cold, buried at the bottom of a pile of luggage, with the plane vibrating and going through a series of drops and rises, and the engines blasting away right over my head like the whole Russian air force with their bombsights lined up on me. I wasn't old enough to remember it, but for the first time in my life, I was able to feel a little sympathy for the poor people of Britain for what they went through during the war, with a little left over for those Nazi bastards who started the whole thing in the first place, and wound up with the shitty end of the stick in their own hands.

It didn't take me long to realize what had happened. Just being in an airborne plane was enough. I didn't need a house to fall on me, just a lot of luggage. I'm sure the head mistresses of those fancy progressive schools I'd attended, who were always extolling my intelligence to Jack, would have peed in their pants with pride at the speed of my reasoning. The plane I had sneaked into, just to catch up on my sleep, had taken off, and right now was flying God knows where with me along as an unpaid passenger, a stowaway, or simply an extra little baggage.

I had always been a prolific reader as a child, usually tales of adventure, more the kind of stuff little boys drooled over than little girls. I guess even then I preferred men to women. The exploits of characters like Blackbeard, Henry Morgan, and Captain Kidd had been my favorites. And thinking of them, I suddenly became scared to death. When I was found, I knew I couldn't be keelhauled, stripped naked in front of the crew and flogged, or locked in a rat-infested brig on bread and water, whenever Cookie remembered to send me any. I was on a plane, not a ship, and none of these things was possible. But I'd never read too much about fliers, and I didn't have the vaguest notion of the procedure they followed when a stowaway was discovered, even an unintentional one like me. Remembering the terrible stories of what pirates did to pretty female captives, I didn't know whether my being a girl would make it any easier for me. But I made up my mind to take advantage of every break I could get. And if it came to the worst, instead of screaming my head off and struggling, I was determined to lie back and enjoy myself, if I possibly could.

After a long time, at least it seemed that way to me, cooped up in the dark of the baggage compartment wondering what would happen to me, the door to the place suddenly opened, letting in too much light too quickly, and making me blink like crazy. Just seeing it open scared me shitless. I knew I finally was going to be discovered. At another time, I probably would have been delighted, because being discovered is the secret dream of every girl. Seventy-five percent of them will admit this right away, and the twenty-five who won't are liars. But in spite of my excellent background, my fancy modern education, and my superior intelligence, I'd never learned the secret of bearing physical pain. As a child, when one of my frustration-free little schoolmates would try to take me apart, I always saved them the trouble by screaming my little head off. Jack, of course, had never really laid a finger on me. Other than for Jim Adams, of the old Bar-Nothing, and that lousy rat-fink, Benjy, no one else had either. But now, I took a couple of extra-deep breaths to build up my lung power, in case the character who was coming in turned out to be the kind who hits first and asks questions afterward.

Crouched in the corner behind an oversized suitcase, I got a pretty good look at him before he spotted me. And piss, shit, and corruption, he was a dream! He was young, he had curly hair, and the kind of face that belonged on the movie screen a lot more than it did in the pilot's compartment of an airliner. Now I had always been a physically attractive person myself. And if I may say so without seeming too stuck-up, after my face, my legs are my bitchiest feature. And when this fellow had rummaged around into my corner of the compartment, I made sure the first thing of mine he laid his eyes on were my legs. I even yanked my skirt up to my pussy so he'd be able to get a pretty good look. And brothers and sisters, he took a pretty good look. Then he raised his eyes to my face, and from what I could see in them, I knew I'd passed the opening test. The first thing he did was slam the compartment door behind him, shutting out the light. Then, he took a flashlight from his pocket and turned it on me, helping himself to a complete look, from the tips of my toes to the top of my head.

"Want me to turn over so you can see the back too?" I asked softly.

"Well, I'll be blowed!" he muttered, sinking back on his heels.

"O.K.," I smiled. "If that's your preference."

"It's a real live doll!" he murmured. "But what's it doing in here?"

"Believe it or not, I was looking for the ladies' room and . . ."

"And?"

"I got trapped."

"In the baggage compartment?"

"Cross my heart, it's the gospel truth!"

Settling himself on the floor, he wriggled into a comfortable position beside me. "Why don't you tell me all about it?"

"O.K.," I shrugged. "The fact is I came into this plane on the ground back in Newark just to take a nap. I didn't know it was going anywhere. Honest!"

"Why a plane?"

"I was an airport and I was tired."

"You mean no one would give a pretty girl like you a place to sleep?"

"That's exactly what I mean," I sighed, resting my head on his shoulder. "I only wanted to sleep and . . ."

"And now?"

"I'm wondering if you have to tell the others I'm in here?"

"Of course," he nodded. "It's regulations."

"Couldn't you overlook them?"

"No! I'm duty-bound to . . . to . . ."

"See more of me?" I finished for him, nibbling at his ear.

"All of you!" he muttered suddenly, taking me in his arms and kissing me until I was breathless. "Inside and out!"

"You the pilot?"

"Co-pilot."

"Where are we going?"

"Charter flight to England."

"England?"

"We're halfway across the Atlantic right now," he nodded, his hands roving all over my body as if he wanted to make sure I was flesh and blood and not a ghost.

Carelessly I dropped my hand into his lap to find out the same thing about him. He was real, all right, stiff as a poker and ready for action. I was delighted at the effect I had on him. And being essentially kindhearted, I unzipped his pants to give him more room, taking his pecker in my hand as it popped out and squeezing it gently. At just about the same moment, his hands found the waistband of my panties, and yanked them all the way down.

"Do we have enough time for this?" I asked curiously.

"Our E.T.A. is about five hours away."

"And yours?"

"The way I feel, about fifteen seconds!"

Flat on the floor by now, we came together with a crash, and we came together as well. Thirty seconds later, I could claim the distinction of being the only girl my age ever to have been fucked in mid-Atlantic on the floor of a loaded baggage compartment. Pussy-petting or fucking, it was the first time in my life I'd ever exploded that quickly, and I didn't know whether it was because of Johnny—his name incidently was Johnny Wilson—or because of my fright at being discovered. But whatever the reason, it was super for both of us. It was a good thing we came that quickly too. Because the way the plane was jumping around in the sky, we probably couldn't have stayed together very much longer. A couple of

100

times, when I was trying to push my hips toward him, the plane fell away beneath us, and my ass end dropped instead. But Johnny was a lad who was able to change direction fast, and we managed to hang together as long as was needed.

A little while later, he closed his pants and got ready to leave. I clutched at him like a drowning person grabbing at a floating log. "What about me?" I demanded.

"I'll be back."

"When?"

"Right after we land at Croydon," he said. Then he reached into his pocket, took something out, and handed it to me. It was a bar of chocolate. "Here! You're probably hungry. This ought to help till we get to London."

I certainly was hungry, the two hamburgers Don had gotten me in Newark being the only food I'd eaten in twenty-four hours. But the idea of landing in a foreign country scared me a whole lot more than the gnawing in my stomach. "What'll I do?" I asked, holding onto his arm. "I don't have a passport or . . . anything!"

He smiled confidently. "I'll take care of everything. I'll just pass you off as a member of the crew."

"But won't the others . . .?"

"Stop worrying," he reassured me. "I've done the same for them many times. A lot of people have the crazy idea that pilots are always screwing the stewardesses on their planes. It's nothing but filthy propaganda. We screw the passengers. It's much more fun and it eliminates unnecessary complications during flights. The stewardesses do the same thing. To make it easier, half of them don't even wear pants on the plane. Sometimes,

101

one of us even brings a friend along for the ride. In this case, I'm bringing you. Skip and Mary Jane owe me a couple of favors. And this flight, they're going to pay off."

"Who's Mary Jane?"

"Our stewardess."

"Is she . . . pretty?"

"She'll do," said Johnny. "Now you stay in here and keep quiet. Take another nap. As soon as the passengers are off, I'll come for you. I'll even bring you Mary Jane's coat so the limey immigration boys'll think you're a member of the crew."

"Gosh!" I murmured with relief. "I don't know how I'll be able to thank you."

"Wait till the two of us get to my flat in London. We'll work on it!"

"Brick!" Johnny sounded almost strangled as he tried to control his breathing, though his lungs were pumping away like crazy. "Help me, for Christ's sake! Help me!"

I was so busy counting the stars embroidered on the tester curtain about the bed, I have to admit I wasn't paying too much attention to what Johnny was doing. I was simply lying back, with my legs wrapped around the backs of his thighs, concentrating on other things . . . like stars. Never before in my whole life had I been in a tester bed. Jack wouldn't have one of the things in the house, calling them symbols of reaction. And all Benjy ever cared about was having a pad, and I mean just that, any place. Having all that fancy junk over my head intrigued me. Johnny was pumping away desperately, his pecker sliding in and out of me, as he tried to work himself to the point

102

of exploding. But since this was the fourth time in the space of a few hours, not counting that time on the plane, he wasn't having much luck, and actually, I wasn't helping him the way I should have been. But after all, how many times in one night can a girl force herself to concentrate just on fucking.

Gasping for breath, Johnny collapsed on top of me, his worn-out pecker quitting him cold. "God-damn it, Brick! What the hell are you doing?"

"Counting the stars on that," I giggled, pointing upwards.

"What a time for arithmetic!"

"But Johnny, there are forty-seven of them on that thing up there. Do you realize—"

"Aw . . . shit!"

Still panting and muttering to himself in disgust, Johnny rolled over on his back, glaring at me as if I were a queen who had just signed the order for his execution. The perspiration was running off the poor darling in rivers. Leaning over, I kissed his lips as effectively as I could, but this time, he was the one who didn't respond.

"I almost had it that time too," he accused me bitterly. "I finally would have been able to say I'd gone four for four. Do you know what that means?"

"No," I whispered, wriggling closer. "What does it mean?"

"It's . . . well, it's like bowling a three hundred game."

"So what?" I complained. "You've rubbed my pussy raw!"

"You just wait till I get my breath back," he threatened angrily. "I'll welt your tail with my belt till it's raw too. Then you'll match, front and back!"

"O.K.," I giggled. "Let's try it tomorrow and see what happens."

"I won't be here tomorrow!"

"Wh-what?"

"We're flying back to the States at noon to pick up another load."

I sat up in the bed with a start, staring down at him. "Holy Toledo! What'll I do?"

"Stay here."

"But . . ."

"The rent's paid till the end of the month," he explained. "I'll be back in three days with more tourists to lap up a little European culture."

"And what do I lap up while you're gone? I haven't a cent!"

"Don't worry. I'll leave you all the cash I have. You'll have food and a place to stay. What more do you want?"

"But what about clothes? That stuff I'm wearing is all I have."

"When I get back we'll go shopping. Day after tomorrow's pay day. I'll be loaded!"

Reassured, I settled back beside him once more, snuggling up tightly and kissing his neck, even nipping at it with my teeth and tasting some of his perspiration. It was salty as hell. "So I'll really be a prisoner of love, huh?"

"Is that bad?"

"What about your nosy landlady? I didn't like the look she gave me when we came in."

"I'll tell her you're my cousin over here on a visit. She won't bother you. Just stay out of her way."

I sighed out loud with relief. And feeling I

104

ought to show him how wonderful he was, particularly after the way I had let him down a little while before, I reached for his pecker, fondling it and exclaiming over it like a precious jewel. But the thing had been worked to a frazzle. And, at the moment, it was limp and wrinkled up to the size of a double peanut. Leaning over him, I brushed the nipple of one of my breasts across his lips. Earlier, I was afraid he'd suck the damn thing off me. But now, the poor darling was so exhausted from fucking, he was fast asleep, and wasn't even aware of what I was doing.

Moving away from him and relaxing on my back in the bed, I ran over in my mind some of the tremendous things that had happened to me in the space of a day and a half. If there was any truth at all in the old wheeze about travel's being broadening, I'd better get busy doing a whole bunch of exercises if I wanted to keep my girlish figure. Because in the last thirty-six hours, I'd come from a cold-water one-room hole in Hoboken to a one-room flat in London, by way of the Newark Airport and a four-engined airliner. At least this one had its own bathroom, which went a long way toward ensuring certain of my comforts. Not bad for a girl who up to a couple of months ago had been the protected ward of one of Manhattan's biggest playboys. Yet here I was now, in the fanciest tester bed I'd ever seen, and the only one I'd ever been in, sharing my blankets with a handsome flier, the way Nell Gwynne, in this same city, had shared hers with Good King Charlie about three hundred years before. It was a little too early to tell whether travel was going to broaden my ass end, but culture was certainly broadening my horizons.

Sometimes, I think nature has her own way of evening things up for everyone. Take Benjy, for example. He was as crummy a rat-fink as ever walked the earth. He was grasping, he was crooked, and he was jockey-sized. Yet he had a flagpole dangling between his legs that more than made up for everything else. Johnny, on the other hand, had looks, education, and breeding. But to make up for all these advantages, nature had handed him just an average-sized pecker. And taking a quick feel of it now, just to check up on my own observations, it was shrunken almost to nothing. Yet I'm sure he could make any red-blooded girl happy with a look, a smile, and maybe two fuckings a night. While Benjy, who had nothing going for him except sex, could fuck the living daylights out of the demandingest pussy this world ever saw, without half trying. And I lay there wondering how many times Jack could deliver in one night, until I fell asleep.

Someday, when I'm older and writing the unexpurgated memoirs of my whole life for posterity, I think I'll devote a chapter or two to reflections on the physical attributes of all the men I've known. And while I have no idea what they'll be like, or even if there will be many, these two, Benjy Brodsky and Johnny Wilson, will rate chapters all of their own.

"Would you mind if I sit next to you?"

I was so lost in my thoughts, it took me a minute or two to realize the man standing in front of my bench in the park was talking to me. Red-faced with embarrassment, I moved closer to one end to leave room for him, meanwhile taking a pretty good look at him to see what he was like. This wasn't because I was becoming more observant. Far from it! In my state of mind, I wouldn't have given a damn if the prime minister's wife suddenly appeared, gamboling naked on the grass. It's simply the way most girls react to most men, in spite of all that ridiculous guff they hand out about not caring one way or the other. The female never lived who didn't size up each new guy in the same way men are always sizing up girls. Maybe not with exactly the same end in mind, but girls like to fuck too. Sex attraction is an instinct born into a woman. And any female who denies it is a shitty liar.

This fellow was dressed very well and very conservatively. He was tall, black-haired, clean-shaven, and attractive. And certainly didn't seem to be the kind of character who hung around public parks trying to pick up unattached girls. But if there is one thing I've learned from my travels of the last few months, it's that the biggest mistake a girl can make is to judge the average guy by appearances alone. Some, who look like butter wouldn't melt in their mouths, can't wait to back a girl into the nearest corner to detail her physical assets, one by one, after close manual examination. While others, who try to give the impression they are fourteen-carat tail-hounds, will treat a girl, and I mean any girl, like she was their sister. So when I moved over, I kept a pretty close watch on this guy to see if I could figure which kind he was going to be.

"Mind if I smoke?" he asked very respectfully.

"I'll join you," I shrugged, reaching out to take one of his cigarettes. Not only did I want it very badly, but I was curious about English cigarettes, having smoked only American ones up to then. He lit it for me with the fanciest lighter I'd ever seen. I was dying to examine it up close, but I decided it wouldn't look right for me to ask. He might get the idea I was trying to get something out of him.

"Not bad," I murmured, blowing out a lungful of smoke. "Not bad at all!"

"You smoke much?"

"Only American cigarettes."

"Why is that?"

"Because I'm American too, I guess."

He shook his head slowly. "If you hadn't told me I'd have never known it. I'd have taken an oath you were a proper English girl taking an outing in the park."

"That's one of the nicest things anyone's ever said to me."

"Don't you like being an American?"

"I wouldn't be anything else. But it's nice for a real Englishman to think I'm English too. It only goes to prove what I've always said . . . girls are girls anywhere in the world."

"You have a very intelligent viewpoint," he murmured. "Everytime you say something, I become happier I sat down next to you."

"Why?"

"I study people," he shrugged. "It's part of my work. And I must admit I've never been this close to an American girl before."

"Didn't you get to know any Waacs during the war?"

"I served in Africa and girls weren't allowed in my regiment. Our colonel was very old-fashioned."

"You poor man," I said. "What is your business?"

"Helping people."

108

"Any particular kind of people?"

"Those who need help."

"What are you, for gosh sakes, a . . . a humanitarian or something?"

"Exactly."

"That's wonderful! I've never met one before!"

He smiled broadly. "By the way, my name is Harry Forsyth."

"I'm Brick MacLean. My real name's Brittania, but with my red hair and all, everyone's always called me Brick."

"Brittania, eh?" he repeated. "So I wasn't wrong. There must be a little English in your background."

"Why do you think I need help?"

"Don't you?"

"I guess I do . . . kind of."

"You seem to be at loose ends," Harry murmured, edging closer to me on the bench. "Almost as if you didn't know what to do next . . . or where you're going."

"Gosh!" I giggled. "How could you tell all that just by looking at me?"

Harry reached over and took my hand. "It's a very special talent."

"Oh."

"Are you all alone in England?"

"Yes."

"Where are your parents . . . your family?"

"I don't have any," I answered softly, deciding not to mention anything about Jack for the moment, or Johnny Wilson either, although I doubted I'd ever see that fink again . . . after what happened at his apartment.

I suppose this would be a good time to explain how I came to be sitting in a park, alone and deserted, without even the money in my pocket to buy a cup of tea. And in England, that's pretty damn well broke. When Johnny had left to fly back to America, he gave me nineteen dollars, all the money he had except for one buck that he needed for carfare after he landed. Nineteen dollars, which comes to about eight pounds in English money, was more than enough to see me through the three days till he returned. So after he'd gone, I felt pretty good, almost as if I were the mistress of my own home as I wandered around his little apartment. I even started rearranging the furniture . . . in my mind, of course. That dream lasted just about fifteen minutes, until his landlady showed up, looking as mean as a hungry tiger about to pounce on her dinner.

"When are you leaving?" she demanded rudely.

"L-leaving?"

"Yes!"

"Not till Johnny gets back . . . at least," I shrugged. "Anyway, he told me the rent's paid till the end of the month."

"So it is, my pretty," she muttered. "But for him, not any little tart he brings home with him to warm the sheets on the bed."

"Who are you calling a tart?" I demanded angrily. "I'll have you know I'm Johnny's cousin . . . from home."

"Cousin my eye!" she sneered. "That young man must have the biggest bloody family in the world. Every time he shows up from the States he's got another relative with him . . . female of course! Last month it was an Italian girl. The time before it was an Oriental. Though I must say you're better looking than any of the others.

But I'm not running a whorehouse. You get your things together and get out!"

I stared at her for a moment, stunned by her words. "But . . . where'll I go?"

"To hell and back for all I care . . . just so long as you're out of my house in ten minutes! If you're still here then, I'll use a broom handle on you and turn you over to the police. They'll know what to do with the likes of you, dearie!"

I looked her over carefully, from head to foot, and decided she was just the kind to do as she threatened. Imagine that Johnny Wilson using me as one of a long list of international bed partners he brought home and lived with a few days at a time. I'd believed him when he said this was the first time. A girl was a fool to trust anybody, aviator or groundhog. Nice manners and a good-looking face certainly didn't make the character behind them any kind of a gentleman. And shoving my nose as high up in the air as I could, and still keep my feet on the ground, I swept out of that crummy little joint as if I were a royal duchess.

By the time I reached the street, I was shaking like a leaf, so I figured I'd better have a cup of coffee to settle myself down a little. I went into the first tearoom I could find. After burning my mouth on as bad a cup of coffee as I'd ever tasted, I realized that all I had with me was American money. But the cashier was very nice about it, and changed my whole nineteen dollars into pounds. Shoving them carelessly into my pocket, I pushed my way through several other customers out into the street. Two blocks later, I put my hand in my pocket and discovered the money was gone. One of those other customers in the tearoom

111

had picked my pocket as clean as a whistle. Whoever it was must have been a smooth operator, too, because I'd never even felt the slightest pull. So from having a paid-up apartment and enough walking-around money for three days, I found myself out on the street without a cent to my name, in a foreign country I was in illegally, with no passport or anything. And what's more, I was a minor. Oh, the police would just love to get their hands on little me. There was nothing left except for me to wander into a nearby park, sit down on a bench, and try to figure out what I should do.

While telling Harry Forsyth I had no family, I watched him out of the corner of my eye, to see if he was the kind I could trust with my full predicament. If he turned me in, I wouldn't be any further up shit creek than I already was. And when he took the news about my being all alone without any surprise or change of expression, I figured I might as well go whole-hog.

"I don't have a passport either," I confessed softly. "Or money . . . or a place to sleep . . . or anything!"

"You really do need help."

"I've never known anyone who needed it more."

"What kind of help did you have in mind?"

"First I need a place to stay," I shrugged. "Then a way to make a little money. At least enough to get me back home."

He relaxed against the back of the bench and smiled cheerfully. "You know, I just might be able to give you a helping hand."

"Really?" I turned the full power of my eyes on him, hoping to make an impression. I guess maybe I did too, because he squeezed my hand a little, which he was still holding in his.

"I think so."

"How?"

"Do you think you can trust me?"

"Oh, yes! I was raised to be an excellent judge of character."

"Good," he smiled. "That will make it easier. It so happens I know a certain lady who's looking for a lovely young girl to be her assistant. And you're certainly that."

"Why . . . thank you."

"Don't thank me. You're very pretty, you know. And from what I can see of it, you've got a knock-out body as well."

"You're not so bad yourself," I giggled. "But what would this lady want me to do? I'm not very experienced."

"She tries to make people happy," Harry explained. "She told me just yesterday she was looking for an attractive young girl to help her . . . someone who could mix well with different sorts of people, who looked and talked like a lady, and was willing to work long hours if she had to. A girl who was willing to go to lengths for money."

"How far?"

"How far what?"

"How far would I have to go?"

"I couldn't say exactly. This lady has her hand in several different types of ventures. It would all depend on which one you'd fit into."

"What business did you say she was in?"

"I didn't. But it's a variation of sociological humanitarianism, together with some sort of physical rehabilitation work. Makes people feel better. Why don't I take you over and introduce you? Then you and she can discuss it between you."

"Swell!" I nodded. "But first, there's something I have to do."

"What?"

"This!" I squealed, throwing my arms around him and kissing him hard. "I knew something would turn up. I just knew it!"

"A regular little Micawber, aren't you?"

There was that name again, the one Jack used to call me all the time, but I still didn't know what it meant. "What's a Micawber?"

"An optimist," grinned Harry. "Also, you're warmhearted."

"Is that bad?"

"On the contrary. It's an important part of the job. But allow me to offer you a tiny piece of advice."

"Oh, yes!"

"Never give everything," he said in a strange kind of way. "Always keep something back in reserve. That way you'll always have a little extra when you need it."

The room I waited in looked like something right out of those *Arabian Nights* stories Wong How used to read to me when I was a little girl, and my guardian was out balling-the-jack with one of the glamour-girl jobs he was always chasing around with. I never did find out if he got to first base with any of them. That breed learns very young to hold out for the highest bid. They're all welfare workers, with the only welfare they're interested in their own. But if he didn't, I know he must have had a hell of a time striking out, trying to make contact with their special curves, because he was always going back for another shot. Anyway, when Harry Forsyth took me to this house and brought me into this room to wait while he told Mrs. Adams I was there, one looked flattened me out like a pancake. There wasn't an honest-to-goodness chair in the whole place. Everything was pillows and divans cut to the floor. It made me remember one of Jack's favorite descriptions about looking like the shithouse in a sultan's harem. And believe me, it fit this joint to a tee. The only things that were missing were the mink-covered chamber pots.

It took me a few minutes to make up my mind where to sit. Everything looked so . . . so luxuriously sinful, I almost went out of my mind with delight. Finally I chose a huge mound of pillows in a corner, and flopped down in a pose I was sure must have been a carbon copy of Cleopatra's as she sailed down the Nile on her purple barge looking for kicks with the local talent. Anyway, I was stretched out on those pillows—they were the most comfortable I'd ever sat on—when a big husky broad, dressed in a violet leotard with perspiration pouring down her ugly face, suddenly was standing over me. The carpets in the room were so darn thick I'd not even heard her come in. And I guess I must have looked about as startled as a hungry alley cat caught in a garbage can by the neighborhood watchdog. But instead of barking and growling, which I'm sure she was capable of doing, this one just stood there, staring down and frowning.

"Yes?" I murmured.

"Madam see you now."

"How about a lift up?" I asked, holding out a hand toward the sweaty woman. "I don't think I can make it without a little help."

She grunted something I couldn't understand. But it must have been "Yes," because grabbing my hand, she yanked me up out of my nest and onto my feet as if I weighed no more than a feather.

"Wow!" I muttered, touching myself all over to make sure I was still in one piece. "I'd hate to tangle with you in a dark alley."

"Why you should?"

"I don't know. But remind me not to try."

She led me through a door, along a hallway, and down a flight of circular iron stairs to the floor below, and then through another door onto a tiny balcony overlooking a tremendous room. At first sight, it looked exactly like the gymnasiums at the schools I'd been sent to. And after a second look, I saw that was exactly what it was—a large gym built in the cellar of the house, outfitted with all the same junk, along with one extra thing. There was a running track—small compared with an outdoor one, of course—around the edge of the room, completely encircling it. Since the physical side of education had never been stressed at any of the progressive institutions I had attended, this was the first indoor track I'd ever seen. There must have been some steam jets in the walls too, because the air was hot, wet, and cloudy. As a matter of fact, the place was so damn cloudy, it took me a minute or two to make out the scene in front of me. Finally I saw that running around the track, more jogging really than running, was a completely naked woman. She didn't seem to have an ounce of fat on her, yet her tits and the cheeks of her ass bounced and jiggled as she moved. And in each of the four corners of the little track, husky broads, dressed like the one who had brought me, were waiting. They held small bundles of switches

116

in their hands, and as the woman passed in front of them, they let her have them across the ass, the legs, or the back. They weren't kidding either, because as she passed in front of me, I could see a whole crisscross of red lines on her skin. And each time they belted her, she let out a yell and picked up the pace for a few steps.

"What kind of a nuthouse is this?" I asked the Amazon who had brought me.

"Combination gymnasium and sauna bath," she grunted. And grabbing my arm, she dragged me off the little balcony over to a door leading into a small room, with lockers lining the walls. Stopping in front of an open one, she pointed first at me and then at the locker. "Take off clothes!"

"Wh-what?"

"Take off clothes!"

"Why?"

"You want talk Mrs. Adams . . . get a job?"

"Yes."

Once again, she pointed to the empty locker. "Take off clothes! Talk together while you run!" Then she looked me over like a friendly St. Bernard and grinned broadly. "I use switches on you too. Make you sting all over. Steam make you sweat. Feel better soon!"

For a moment, I was speechless. Then the power of my tongue came back with a rush. "If you think I'm going to strip and run around the track with that woman while you whip me you're nuttier than I think you are!"

She frowned, puzzled by my reluctance. "Is good for young girl. Learn in Finland. Healthy! Sweat and whip! Make feel good all over!"

"How do I get out of here?" I yelled.

Realizing I would make no move by myself to

get undressed, she grabbed me and stripped me down to the skin, putting my clothes carefully in the locker, and handling me just as if I were a baby. When she was finished, she looked me over critically, moving her hands over my body and touching me here and there. "Little girl," she muttered. "Nice legs . . . backside . . . but too small titty. Need exercise. Olga fix. Olga teach you!"

Holding my arm in her huge paw with a grip of iron, she pulled me out into the gym toward the running track, on which I could see Mrs. Adams still going around, still being whipped by the waiting women in the corners, and still yelping each time their switches touched her, her white hide even more striped now than before. At the edge of the running surface, Olga suddenly shoved me out, helping me get started with a stinging wallop right across the ass. Before I could even turn around to swear at her, Mrs. Adams came along. Taking my hand, she pulled me with her until I was jogging by her side. At the first corner, I tried my best to duck. But Olga was waiting with a big grin on her ugly face, and curled the switches around my companion to catch me flush on the ass. I yelped and jumped as they stung my skin, making Mrs. Adams giggle.

"What are you running here?" I gasped, already panting from the exertion. "A concentration camp . . . or a reform school?"

"I like a girl with spirit," she smiled. "But you're badly out of shape. A youngster like you should be able to run around here for hours at a time."

"What are we training for . . . the Olympic games?"

"A tougher business than that," she said slowly,

118

her tits bouncing a lot more than mine because they were bigger. Then she dropped back a step for a minute to look me over. "You've a lovely figure, my dear."

"Your Amazon, Olga, didn't think so," I grumbled as we jogged along. "First she told me I had no tits, and then she smacked me as hard as she could. The mark will never go away."

"Of course it will," grinned Mrs. Adams. "That only means she likes you. But you know these Scandinavians. Everything has to be king-size to please them."

"What started you on this health kick, anyway?"

"You're American, aren't you?"

"Yes."

"Your American physical fitness program," she shrugged. "I like it. It showed good thinking."

"Really?"

"It should be made a must for everybody. Good health is vital."

"For what?"

"For living. And certainly for the way you'll have to live if you work for me."

"I don't understand," I panted. By now, my skin was as striped as hers, and I was getting my second wind. Also, the stinging felt wonderful. "Harry told me you were a humanitarian. I didn't know it was so tough to give things away. I always figured that was easy."

"It all depends on what you're giving," she smiled. "I've found people appreciate things more if they have to pay for them."

"What business are you in?"

"Sex!"

"Sex?"

She nodded seriously. "Yes. I pander to the idiosyncrasies of the upper classes."

"Is that what they call fucking in England?"

"Oh, we go far beyond that. Plain fucking is only for peasants. Our clients insist upon more individually expressive and sophisticated games."

"But why only the upper classes?"

"They're the only ones who'll pay for it. Those Labourites are as tight-fisted as misers. And I am not a philanthropist . . . though Harry insists on calling me a humanitarian."

"Do they have many idiosyncrasies?"

"Who?"

"The upper classes?"

"The bloodiest you ever heard of," she giggled heartily. "And they all come to me because my girls are trained to indulge them."

"In fucking . . . and beyond?"

"Mostly beyond."

"How far?"

"My dear, every one of my assistants is an artist in copulation, oral stimulation, and masochism."

"I know what copulation is, but the rest of that . . ."

"Fucking, sucking, and whipping."

"Gosh!"

"Do you think you'd like to be one of us?"

"Uh-huh!"

"Good!" Mrs. Adams smiled admiringly at me. "You won't be sorry, I can promise you that. You certainly have all the physical requirements, and Olga will teach you everything you have to know. From the way she keeps watching you, I can tell she's taken a great liking to you."

"I'm glad," I smiled, tenderly feeling my sitting area. It still stung like crazy where she had smacked it. "I probably wouldn't have any rear end left if she didn't."

Taking my hand once again, she slowed us down to a walk, going through a whole series of deep-breathing exercises at the same time. "I think we're ready for our rubdowns," she explained. "We'll have them together. That way I can explain our setup while the girls work on us."

Climbing onto the table, I kept one eye on Olga's preparations and the other on my brand-new boss. "There are a couple of things I'd like to ask?"

"What?"

"Is the money good?"

"There isn't another establishment anywhere that pays a higher rate for piecework."

"And the work . . . is it hard?"

"Easy," she smiled. "Our clients are among the best people in the country. Some have even been members of the government. And they all bathe regularly, you know. Of course, sometimes their games do get to be a little uncomfortable."

"How uncomfortable?"

"That all depends on the girl. But I'm sure you'll be in great demand. They'll go mad just to whip that cute little bottom of yours. It's so firm and juicy. And to have you whip theirs. They find it a little embarrassing with an older woman."

"Everyone'll just want to . . . wh-whip me?"

"Mostly."

"But you said they were the best people. Has fucking gone out of style in England?"

"Hardly. But this bunch has spent their lives riding to the hounds. I guess they don't feel com-fortable without their whips."

"Tallyho the fox and all that jazz, huh?"

"Exactly."

"Gosh!"

"Just look at it this way, my dear. Everything has its compensations. They'll have to pay much higher fees for you, and we'll split those right down the middle . . . fifty-fifty!"

"I like that part of it," I murmured, still a little scared at the whole idea. "And maybe I can get them to change their diets."

"If anyone can, you're the one to do it."

"Then it's a deal!"

"Lord Ashley is waiting below, mum."

I nodded to the maid in the dressing-table mirror and smiled. "Thank you, Agnes."

She left and I went back to making sure my eye shadow was deep enough, and my mascara just right. Finishing that, I got up to pose before the full-length mirror. Entirely naked, I was able to give myself a complete once-over. My figure certainly had improved. Olga knew what she'd been talking about when she said she'd show me how to build up my tits. Not that they would ever be uddery, or anything like that. No matter what I did, short of an operation, they'd always be on the petite side. But at least they were approaching a respectable size, they were firm, and they filled out the front of my clothes just enough to make me more interesting to male eyes. My waist was small, my hips swingy, and I was sure my face, always pretty, was now sophisticated enough to please any man. Deep down inside, I wondered, as I always had, whether it would attract Jack, still the only man I ever wanted to attract that way. But it didn't look as if I would find out.

Craning my neck to look at my rear view in the glass, I was glad to see that all the signs of my last session with one of my clients had disappeared, leaving my skin smooth and unmarked. I patted my bottom gently and sighed. I don't know what it is with Englishmen, but every one of them likes to whip the ass end of a girl before fucking her. The girls in the place who were English told me it was a leftover from the glorious days of knighthood, when they all rode around poking at each other with long lances. They called it jousting. Today, they still go in for the same thing, except that now they try to poke pussies with their peckers. I don't know whether those other girls were right or not. But I do know every one of those characters gets a charge just holding a whip in his hands. Some even like the feel of it on their own skins, used by the girl they want to fuck. It must be something in their culture, passed down from the Norman Conquest, because even the army officers over here walk around with fancy little swagger sticks in their hands. I wondered whether they ever used them on each other, but I never had the nerve to ask.

Roger Ashley was young, he was rich, he was handsome, and he was off his nut about me. But best of all, he wasn't too bright. So when we had our little parties, which happened no less than three times every week, I convinced him, if he got that crazy urge, to spank me with his hand instead of lashing me with his whip. I told him it excited me more that way, and the dope swallowed it, hook, line, and sinker. That way, unless he got carried away with what he was doing, the marks never stayed around more than a couple of hours, and I was able to take care of any other business that came my way. It's goddamned uncomfortable trying to get sexy with a guy when you've got an ass full of welts. As a matter of fact, it's impossible. And I found out very quickly that the extra money it earned me never equaled what I lost by being temporarily retired from the action. So it didn't take very long for the word to get around town that the little American at Mrs. Adams' wouldn't hold still for the usual. The boys found out I'd put up with being hand-smacked for the right price, but I wasn't going to stand for any of that whipping shit from anyone. And that went for two different characters from the Royal Family too, whom I chased out of my room when they started swishing their bats, as they called them. Remembering these fellows, sometimes I wonder if the Queen and the Royal Princesses stand around as much as they do at receptions because they can't sit down. I wish I knew one of them well enough to ask.

I have to admit my life as a fancy whore wasn't all it's cracked up to be. I got my share of proposals, of course, mostly to be set up in an apartment of my own, to be the exclusive possession of the guy doing the setting up. But I discouraged these right away. The only guy I knew I'd be a private concubine for lived in America, and he didn't seem too anxious to find me. But my work sure brought me into contact with a collection of kooks. One guy never took his hat off, no matter what else he wasn't wearing. If you think this isn't upsetting, try fucking sometime with a character wearing a bowler, as the English call them, and see if you can keep from laughing. This nut reminded me of the hero in Western movies, whose hat never comes off, even when he's being

124

punched around by a bunch of assorted villains. I tried my darnedest to knock it off everytime we fucked. I never did find out if he glued it on, but no matter how I bounced him, the damn thing never moved an inch. Then there was the kook who always brought his private soapbox with him. He'd make me wear blue-jean stretch pants, while he stood naked on the box in the middle of the room and lectured me on the evils of prostitution. He had a pretty good spiel too, because a couple of times he started getting to me. Then he'd sit on the box, pull my pants down, bend me over his lap, and tickle my ass till I giggled like a loon. Never once did he take me to bed afterward. I guess he was just an old ass-tickler. When he had enough, he'd pat me on the head, tell me to be a good girl, get dressed, and leave.

But Lord Ashley was the best by far. He rarely smacked me very hard. Sometimes I think he only did it once in a while because he felt he had to be true to the heritage of an English gentleman. These characters are great ones for being loyal to their class. To them, anything less is treason. But I must say he liked fucking better than smacking. And best of all, he liked to fuck me, which was not only enjoyable but good for my income. He had more money than he knew what to do with, and was always bringing me fancy little presents like French perfume, sexy underwear, and once even a diamond wristwatch. And he was the only one I ever took anything from, other than my regular fee, which was pretty damn good by itself. I already had a good little nest egg tucked away, more than enough to take me home. But I was a minor, I didn't have a passport, I couldn't explain being in the country, and I was having myself a ball and wasn't in any hurry to leave.

Every day I spent a couple of hours in the gym, running around the track, and getting belted with those darn switches. I even got to like it, the exercise, the sweating, the stinging, and the whole bit. The ice-cold shower at the end took a little getting used to, but after a while, even that got to be fun. But it must have been a healthy pastime, because I never felt so well in my life, and I had the staying power of a marathon runner. Olga practically adopted me. She was the only one in England I ever told my real age. And when she heard I was only sixteen, she took over the job of being a mother to me. She waited on me, she rubbed me down after the gym, she dressed me, she undressed me. Honest to God, I think she'd even have wiped my bottom in the john if I'd let her. Sometimes, though, her protectiveness got to be a pain. When she thought I'd worked enough, she'd come right into my room, shoo everyone out, and put me to bed, whether I wanted to go or not. She was a real nut about rest and health. And when I'd blow my cork and scream at her, she'd just grin at me with that ugly kisser and go right ahead with what she was doing, as if I hadn't been saying a word. There were times, of course, when I was glad she was around. Whenever I'd have a customer, she parked herself at the door. And if he started to get out of hand, she'd take the guy apart, limb from limb, before tossing him out.

Slipping into a pair of shorts and a bikini top, the kind of thing Lord Ashley liked best on me, I hurried to get ready. Finally, after a last look in the

126

mirror to make sure everything was O.K., I rang the buzzer which told Agnes below to show him up. In Mrs. Adams' place, each girl had her own apartment. It was almost like living at home and entertaining boy friends. It made for a lot of privacy too. And with the room all soundproofed, no one could hear what went on in the next apartment. The girls could scream and moan their heads off—some did, thinking it pleased their partners—or whoop it up all they wanted, without having to worry about their neighbors. The only time the boss ever showed her face, except to a favored few, was after the last customer had left. Then she'd visit each one of us in turn, to check over our books and collect her fifty percent. With clothes on, Mrs. Adams was a very feminine-looking female, much more like somebody's aunt than the most successful madam in London. But I know I'd never have dared try to hold out on her. A couple of the girls did while I was there, and I never saw either of them after they were caught. I don't know exactly what happened to them. But after all the scary rumors we heard, no one ever tried it again.

"Lass?" Roger called as he hurried through the door. "Where are you?"

Catching sight of him, I stopped dead in my tracks. "Roge!" I squealed. "You darling! You did it! You kept your promise!"

Lord Ashley was dressed in kilts. Also, he'd had too much to drink. One look at his face was enough for anyone to see that. But ever since I'd found out he was a Scotsman, I'd been badgering him to let me see what he looked like in his national costume.

"Family dinner," he muttered, embarrassed at

the way I was staring. "Head of the clan, you know. Had to wear full regalia. Couldn't let anyone down."

"I should hope not," I giggled, walking around him to enjoy the view from all angles. Having catered to his yen rather steadily, I was very familiar with what he looked like naked. But this was the first time I'd ever seen him half-naked while he was all dressed. "You're a bit of all right, milord! But don't sit down yet. There's something I've got to do."

"What?"

"All my life I've wondered how a guy feels when he puts his hand up a girl's skirt."

"Haven't the foggiest. Never tried it."

Moving up to him quickly, I shoved my hand under the front of his skirt and ran right into his pecker, at the moment all soft and squishy. "Hmm! So it's true!"

"What?"

"Scots really don't wear anything under that darn skirt."

" 'Course not! It would only get in the way."

"I know."

"How?"

"I've heard what happens up in the heather when a braw lad takes a bonny lassie for a walk."

"True," he admitted. "Scotland's the most fornicating country on earth. But how else can the poor devils stay warm? Half the time it rains, and the other half it's foggy!"

"I once knew a psychiatrist in New York who insisted masturbation would save the world from disease and overpopulation. Wouldn't that keep them warm less dangerously?"

"A Scot who'd run from that kind of danger

must be three-quarters English. But it wouldn't work in the Highlands. Too lonely!"

Stripping off my shorts and halter, I giggled as his pecker suddenly became erect and pushed out the front of his skirt. "Doesn't that ever get embarrassing?" I asked, pointing at the bulge. "Suppose it happened at the wrong time?"

"Too cold! Anyway, that's how they separate the men from the boys in the Highlands."

"Bullshit!"

"I mean it. When they have a get-together, the men all stand around watching the lassies do the fling by themselves. Then, the one whose skirt sticks out the farthest gets his pick of the litter."

"I thought the men spent their time tossing the caber?"

Dropping his kilt to the floor, he held out his pecker toward me. "This is the only caber I ever tossed."

In a minute, he had everything else off as well. And picking me up in his arms, he carried me over to the bed. "We play another game I've always liked better," he grinned. "Are you ready to kiss the king?"

"What's that?"

"When the fellow with the biggest chooses his lass, the first thing she has to do, when they're alone, is put her lips to it. It's called kissing the king."

"Does he ever kiss the queen?"

"If he's a true Scotsman!"

"O.K., milord," I murmured. "I'm lowering my drawbridge. As soon as the greetings are finished, I'll be expecting you in the main hall of the queen's castle."

"Tallyho!"

People are always talking about getting started off on a lucky streak, when everything they do turns out right. I don't know very much about it, maybe because I've never been very interested in gambling. And most of the characters you hear blowing off are card players or horse players, and even stock-market players. But I first began to get an idea of what they meant when everything started coming up roses for me too. Or, at least, I thought it was. Up to then, I certainly wouldn't have won any medals for being lucky, or sensible either, as a matter of fact. I'd managed, without any help from anyone, to go from a luxury apartment the East Side of New York to a one-room cold-water flat in Hoboken, to a tiny flat in London, and straight into the fanciest whorehouse in town. I don't think anybody, no matter what kind of screwed-up mind they had, would call that exactly improving oneself. If it isn't going right into the shithouse, I don't know what else it could be. Then, four weeks ago, my best regular, Roger Ashley, decided he didn't like coming to a professional house almost every night in the week. He liked me, he liked the way I fucked, but he didn't like what it would do to his reputation if the word got around that he was spending so much of his time at Mrs. Adams'. So he sold me on the idea of setting up for myself, in a private apartment, where I'd be free to do anything I wanted, or entertain others when he wasn't around. Actually, he didn't have to be too super a salesman to get me to agree. I was getting a snootful of spreading my legs and getting my ass smacked by every Tom, Dick, and Harry who could afford it, with half the take going to someone else. And as long as Roge didn't expect me to be his private possession only, I finally let him convince me.

Mrs. Adams was fit to be tied. As a matter of fact, she turned into a raging tigress right in front of my eyes. I'd always thought, up to that time, that regardless of what she was faced with, she could never be anything but a complete lady. But when she found out I was leaving to go into an apartment of my own, she raised the roof right off the joint, even though I explained I had no intention of offering her any competition. Then when Olga told her she'd be going with me, that's when the shit really hit the fan. She busted out with a string of four-letter Anglo-Saxon words that left me spellbound. And for a product of progressive education, with its emphasis on free expression for everybody, that was a real compliment. I'd always thought I was a pretty good hand at it myself. But after listening to her spout off for a few minutes, I knew I was a nothing. I heard myself called more kinds of cocksucker than I ever knew existed. She told Olga off, and when Roge showed up, she told him off most of all. But like all the characters who live in this country, there are times he has more ice water in his veins than blood. I guess the reason these people use the word bloody so much is because they don't have enough of their own. Anyway, he just stood quietly, looking at her with a very uppity expression on his face, and let her go as far as she liked. Then, when she ran out of breath, he bowed very coldly, and asked me if I was ready to leave, ignoring the woman as if she didn't exist.

A couple of hours later, I found myself in this dreamy apartment in a fancy section of town. Roge had rented it a couple of days before. And for the first time in months, I was living in more than a one-room flat. This one had six, and they were all mine. The first few times I looked around the place, I had to pinch myself to see if Brick MacLean really was the girl living here, or if it was a stranger I didn't know. Now, getting dressed for the first real party I was giving, I was in seventh heaven. My guest list included, along with Roger Ashley, the American ambassador, a high member of the Austrian government, and the prime minister of one of those new African countries, who happened to be in London for a state visit, and knew Roge from having worked for him as a porter on a safari he'd made several years before.

I had arranged for three girls to be included, one for each of my guests. I, of course, would be with Roge, and naturally I invited the prettiest ones I could, from a group I personally knew wouldn't draw the line at anything the men might get a notion to try. While Mrs. Adams' girls always worked privately, we did gossip among ourselves, and sometimes even compared notes in our spare time. And it wasn't too long before I had a pretty good idea who did what best. And for this night, I'd gone to a lot of trouble and extra expense getting four sets of little horse's tails and tiny whips made, exactly like the ones Dr. Freund had used on me the one time in his office we'd really fucked. I'd never told anybody about that game, particularly since I'd made such a thing about not being whipped. But I figured it could be the high point of the evening, depending on how things went. After all, I had a reputation to uphold, and a good hostess always tries to provide something extra for her guests. Roge, I knew, would love it. The

132

American ambassador had been a famous horseman in his younger days, and would be able to hold his own on the back of a naked girl without any trouble. The Austrian probably would too, the way Austrians were always bragging about their Spanish riding school in Vienna. It was the African prime minister who gave me the biggest headache. I didn't know if he knew one end of a horse from the other, and I wasn't too sure how the girls would take to him, Roge having warned me he was as black as the ace of spades. But I was sure he'd know how to use the little whip. And I'd have bet my last cent that if he was like other blacks, he'd get a special kind of charge out of whipping a white girl on the bare behind.

The evening started out famously. The men seemed to be delighted with the girls, and I knew the whole thing would be a great success when I learned five shakers of martinis had been used up before we even sat down to dinner. They were all in a high old mood, and during the dinner, the wine kept flowing like water. The only thing that really surprised me was the way that African got along with a knife and fork. I'd been a little afraid about his being able to handle himself at the dinner table, particularly as Roge told me he'd been such a lousy porter on the safari. But I guess he must have watched the people he worked for when they were out on the trail, because he didn't try to eat with his knife, and he didn't stab his tongue even once with the fork. What's more, the girls were nuts about him on sight. I have to admit he looked a little like a Zulu ready for the warpath, or whatever the hell they call it in Africa. But he was quiet and well mannered.

Unlike at most English dinners, the other girls

and I didn't leave the table to the men after dessert while they did a little serious drinking. We stayed right with them. While I don't drink much of anything, never having developed a taste for alcohol, the other girls kept right up with their partners, belt for belt. And when the brandy was finished, it began to look as if the party was about to begin. We danced all the latest dances, the watusi, the swim, the frug, and the monkey. I don't think we missed any of them. And the funniest thing was when the eight of us started to do them naked. Seeing all those ambassadorial and ministerial peckers, black and white, jumping up and down in rhythm, while four sets of tits also began jiggling in time to the music, was an absolute scream. All it would have taken to make everything perfect would have been some rock 'n' roll drummer, naked, banging away on his white man's version of the tom-toms. I was sorry I didn't have a movie camera to put it all on film, not that it would have been allowed, of course. These fellows were much too careful about blackmail, should such pictures ever fall into the wrong hands.

When it looked like the men were about ready to take the girls into other rooms for some inspired fucking, I decided the time was ripe for my horsie game. And because my guests were such important people, I christened it, on the spur of the moment, with a name in keeping with their backgrounds and positions.

"Anybody want to play black bottom?" I called out as loudly as I could, to make myself heard over the noise.

"What's that?" asked the American ambassador.

134

"Why black bottom?" chorused the girls curiously.

I couldn't help giggling. "Because after a couple of games, your bottom will be black for days."

"Then what are we waiting for?" they shrieked, past caring about anything but fun. "Let's play!"

Dragging out my equipment, I tied horse's tails around each of the girls' hips, and gave each of the men a little whip. We decided, since there would be four teams, to run our races in heats, two against two, with the winners facing each other in the finals. While the men cleared the furniture out of the way, we got ready for the first heat. The floor was carpeted, wall to wall, so no one had to be concerned about skinned knees, or bruises and scrapes, in case one of the girls bucked and threw her rider. And since it was my game, Roge and I entered the first heat against the African prime minister and his girl, a very blonde and white-skinned example of Nordic supremacy. The other four got back into a corner to keep out of the way, and acted like the rooting section at a football game back home. The course was ten laps around the room, which allowed plenty of time for each girl to be whipped into a frenzy.

Being the only experienced player, I jumped into the lead right away. But that didn't keep Roge from flailing away at my bare bottom with his tiny whip till my ass felt like it had been stung by a thousand angry bees. The African's girl took a pretty good beating too, worse than I did as a matter of fact, because she kept collapsing under the weight of her rider. But that black man caught on real fast. He lashed away at his girl-horse until she got back to her hands and knees and took off after Roge and me. After four laps, that poor girl

135

was shouting and screaming from the whipping, and straining as hard as she could to catch up. I was too excited to yell much at that moment, but I made up my mind to speak to Roge when the heat was over about the way he kept whipping me even though we were about six lengths in front. The noise in the room was tremendous, with the riders whooping, the girl-horses yelling, and the rooting section in the corner cheering us on like mad. Then, just as Roge and I started our last lap, ten lengths ahead by now, with my rear looking as if it had been a battleground for a tick-tack-toe tournament, and the other girl's in even worse shape, the doors suddenly burst open and a squad of bobbies, led by a big burly sergeant, came rushing into the room.

Calling what we were doing the most revolting exhibition of hysterical masochistic sadism—this cop must have studied psychology in his spare time—he'd ever seen, the sergeant ordered us all to get dressed at once, and prepared to bundle the eight of us into police cars for a trip to the local pokey. When Roger pointed out the rank and position of the men involved, he became greatly embarrassed. But he couldn't let them go without letting us girls go too, and that was one thing he wasn't about to do, come hell or high water.

The Austrian official started moaning openly about what mamma was going to say when the story broke in the newspapers, which it surely would. Roge was stony-faced. The American ambassador shrugged and said he was tired of the diplomatic rat race anyway, and would be happy to get back to his horse-breeding farms. The only one who was really enjoying himself was the African prime minister. It couldn't have been because he didn't understand what was happening. But I suppose the closer a man is to primitive living, the less he worries about misfortune. I know he wasn't stupid. And yet with the broad grin on his face, he looked exactly like that big black gorilla that used to frighten me, as a child, in the zoo in Central Park. All he needed was a banana to be a carbon copy.

About to climb into one of the police cars, I asked the sergeant who tipped the cops off. "Had the neighbors complained about the noise?"

"No, ma'am!"

"Then who?"

"A party named Mrs. Adams called in," he muttered. "She told us you were putting on a series of Roman orgies, and she insisted we put a stop to them. She sounded like a proper lady, too. And she was right. I never saw a more flagrant exhibition of sexual fornication in my life!"

"Sergeant," I giggled. "Is there any other kind?"

"White girls with a black man. It's disgraceful!"

"I thought the English didn't believe in racial discrimination!"

"We don't! Certainly not in the jungle once in a while, when a man can't help himself. But right in London among your own kind, it's uncivilized!"

"By any chance, sergeant, did your family move here from Alabama?"

"Into the car with you," he muttered hoarsely, giving me a gentle nudge from behind. "It will go better for all of you if you make no trouble before you see the magistrate!"

Staring through the barred window of my "room" in juvenile prison, I began to have a few serious

137

doubts concerning that lucky streak I'd been bragging about just a few weeks before. Jack had always told me, when I was a little girl and believed
every word he said, that it never paid a fellow to
be a pioneer. All he could expect was to get his
ass shot full of arrows by the unfriendly natives.
And at that moment, I was convinced that my ass
was the one that was going to be presented to the
Indians for target practice. When good luck comes
to a person, generally it shows up a little bit at a
time. But bad luck always comes in bunches. And
believe me, I was in it up to my eyes, my ears,
and my nose.

When we arrived in front of the police station
the night they raided my apartment and caught us
playing black bottom steeplechase in the parlor, a
kind of riot suddenly broke out down at the end
of the street. The timing was so perfect, a suspicious character would have been sure it had
been prearranged. Unfortunately, I was in a
slightly different situation from the others. As far
as the men were concerned, the British government would never actually allow any of them to
be officially arrested. They might be asked to
leave the country as quietly as they could, but at
least they wouldn't have to face a magistrate in
open court and explain what they were doing in
my apartment naked, in the company of four
naked females. But then, diplomats always get
away with murder as far as the laws of any
country are concerned. Not that an explanation
was really necessary. Englishmen like to fuck as
much as anyone else. And no matter how such a
shindig starts, it always winds up with fucking.
That much my travels had taught me. The other
three girls, of course, were old hands at being

138

pinched. They'd been there before, they knew the ropes, and beyond a small fine or maybe a thirty-day jugging, they weren't going to get into too much hot water. But I was in a different class entirely. First, I was a minor. Second, I was in the country illegally, and had no passport or anything else to show who I was or where I'd been born. And third, by admitting the first two, I indicted myself as a runaway. Piss, shit, and corruption! Of the eight of us, I was the only one liable to get the rope. And when that commotion started down the street, and the cops who were taking us in ran down there to see what it was all about, I decided very quickly that my first duty was to my own skin. Let the rest of those characters, Lord Roger Ashley included, take care of themselves, because that was exactly what little Brick was going to do too. I may have missed a lot during my formative years because of certain gaps in my education. But that didn't mean I was any moron. Maybe I couldn't read Virgil in the original Latin. As a result of the fancy system of word recognition I'd been taught, I had enough trouble with English. But I could smell danger to me like a bloodhound. So when those cops went one way, I went the other, as fast as my young legs could carry me.

Before I knew where I was headed, I found myself at the docks along the river, where a number of ships were tied up. From the look of a couple of them, and the activity going on all over them, it seemed, even to a landlubber like me, that they were getting ready to take off for somewhere. Just watching the loading, the stowing, and the hustle sort of got to me. And that's when the wonderful idea hit me. Why shouldn't I sail on one of them? The cops would surely be looking for me, there wasn't a soul in London I gave a rap about except Olga, and there wasn't anything I could do about her now. So why not? Only this time I was a little smarter than when I'd flown here as a stowaway from Newark. And I was getting awfully tired of having no identification. But this time I'd sign on as a regular member of the crew. And when we got where we were headed, I'd be able to take off without a worry, and maybe with a few bob to jingle in my pockets as I walked away. But first, I had to get rid of my clothes.

Scouting around the docks in the darkness, I found an open locker with a pair of ragged pants, a dirty shirt, and a pair of beat-up men's shoes. Thank the Lord the guy who owned them was on the small side! Holding the things up against me, I was sure they would fit well enough for me to get by. Then, underneath a pile of rubble, I found an old cap. It wasn't much, but it would serve to hide my hair till I could cut most of it off. And for the first time since I'd met her, I was glad Olga's exercises hadn't made my tits too big. Maybe an old sea captain could be fooled into thinking I was a boy. I didn't know if it would work, but it was certainly worth a try. Otherwise, I was a lead-pipe cinch to end up in jail. And while I had always been the kind of girl who was anxious to learn new things, I figured a stretch in the pokey was one thing I could do without.

Changing my clothes in a corner and leaving mine in the empty locker, I strolled up the gangplank of the nearest ship with a rolling strut, as if I didn't have a care in the world, and asked for the captain. He turned out to be a grizzled old veteran of the sea and as busy as a one-armed paperhanger, who took me at face value without

140

even a glance, had me sign on as a cabin boy, and sent me forward to see the doc. Everything in this country was being nationalized by the new Labour government, and the health of its sailors had become a question of tremendous political importance. Safeguarding the crew members from disease had become the duty of the National Health Service. The sailors, of course, were all for it, since the doctors were socialized, and everything was for free. And if the treatment wasn't all it was cracked up to be, it didn't cost the shipowners a cent, and the men weren't any worse off than before.

Heading forward, I found the doctor without any trouble. He was putting his equipment away as I came along, having already finished with the rest of the men. He looked me over with a pretty sharp eye.

"What have we here?"

"Cabin boy, sir," I muttered, trying to make my voice sound deeper than it was.

"Well, come closer, lad! Come closer! My eyes aren't so good anymore and I have to examine you."

"Oh, that won't be necessary, sir." I touched my cap in a gesture of respect. "I'm in good shape, sir. Tip-top shape."

"No doubt," he nodded slowly, squinting at me. "You certainly look as if you've been getting plenty of food and rest. But there's one thing I still have to do."

And turning around, he reached into his bag, took out a hypodermic syringe, and half filled it from a tiny vial of colored liquid. Then he turned back to me.

"Let down your britches, lad!"

"What?"

"Let down your britches!"

"I certainly will not! What do you think I am?"

"Come, come!" the doc smiled, holding up the syringe. "You've got me wrong, lad. I'm just going to shoot you with this stuff. It's the law! Don't be bashful. One cheek for cholera and the other for typhoid. It's for your own good . . . compliments of the government."

"Does the law say you can't shoot me in the arm?" I demanded suspiciously.

I wasn't about to take my pants down. Besides, my ass end was still all marked up from Roge's whipping me in the black bottom steeplechase, and I didn't want to put any ideas into his head. He might be an old man, but he was an Englishman too, and a girl couldn't be too careful who she showed her ass to in this country.

"Regulations say in the butt, lad," he growled. "Now drop them down. I haven't got all night."

"I'll . . . I'll take them in the arm, sir," I said defiantly, rolling up my sleeve in preparation.

"MacTavish!" the doctor called out suddenly.

A huge hairy man came lumbering in, almost out of nowhere. "Aye, sor?"

"The lad's bashful about letting down his britches," the doctor grinned, gesturing at me. "Lend him a hand."

Before I could even get out one yelp, the big jerk had grabbed me, and stripped down my pants till they hung around my ankles. Then, lifting me around the middle, with my face against his chest, he held me out, ass first, toward the doctor. "Here you be, doc," he chuckled. "Stick the little bugger good!"

Immediately, the doctor noticed the crisscrossed

142

whip marks on my skin. "I see you've been a naughty lad," he muttered, reaching out his hand to touch the marks on my bottom. The only way I can figure it is that he must have been made suspicious by the soft roundness of my ass. Because suddenly, without a word of warning, his fingers shot between my legs and ended up right in my pussy.

"Hey!" I shouted, kicking out with both legs, knocking the syringe out of his hand with one foot, and letting him have the other right in the pit of his stomach. "Your government may supply you bastards with everything, but my pussy isn't free!"

Then, twisting away from the stunned Mac-Tavish, I kicked off the pants that were entangling my ankles and headed for the door. But the big Scot stuck out an arm to stop me, and somehow managed to grab himself a handful of the back of my shirt. The material must have been older than I figured, because it split down the front and I ran right out of it. Except for the cap on my head and the shoes on my feet, I was as naked as I could be. I ran like all the devils in hell were after me. And two of them were—MacTavish and that old doctor.

Out on deck, I made straight for the gangway with the two of them right at my heels, the three of us yelling and screeching at the top of our lungs.

"What the hell's going on down there?" The captain's bellow came down from the bridge in the night air.

"It's the new cabin boy, sor," panted Mac-Tavish.

"What about him?"

"He's a . . . a girl, sor!"

"What?"

"And he's . . . I mean, she's as naked as the day she was born!"

The captain's figure hung over the bridge railing. "What the hell's wrong with that doctor? Can't that lousy Socialist government send us one who knows the difference between a boy and a girl?"

By this time, I was down the gangplank and running along the dock into the welcome shelter of the darkness, with the white skin of my ass end making me stand out like a cottontail rabbit down its whole length. And completely bare is no way for a girl to try to run through a man's world, at least if she hopes to come away in anything like the same condition she got in. It didn't take two seconds for the news to be shouted, from ship to ship and pier to pier, that a naked broad was running loose in the area. Almost immediately, the dock became jammed with sailors and stevedores all hunting for little me, hoping to get a look, a feel, or even more, if they could manage it before being swamped in the stampede. Then, just as I thought there was an even chance I'd be able to avoid them and get away free, I had to go and run right into the arms of a bobby, who was hurrying toward the docks to investigate the wild commotion.

Hardly twenty minutes later, with a blanket wrapped around me in place of the clothes I'd left behind, I was here in this juvenile detention home. It seems that while I'd been busy trying to make a getaway, the police had brought Olga in for questioning about the orgy, and found out from her that I was only sixteen. I really couldn't blame her too much. The poor woman may have been

144

built like an Amazon, but she'd been scared shit-less by all those uniforms, and blabbered every-thing she knew. So there was nothing left for me to do but spill the whole story of how I came to be in England. The only thing I held back was the name of the pilot who'd helped me, and the air-line he flew for. I knew I was in plenty of hot water, but I couldn't see any point in pulling Johnny Wilson in after me. Besides, he hadn't known my real age either.

The newspapers had a regular field day. It was a real juicy scandal, and there were some big names involved. I'll have you know the story even got three paragraphs in the London *Times.* All the reporters wanted pictures, and I posed as often and as prettily as I could. But those headlines! Why, they made the tabloids back home seem almost like church periodicals. And of course, since I was an American girl, our papers picked the whole thing up right away. Jack, who never went home at night in his life without the *Daily News,* saw the story and the pictures and wired the embassy first, to intervene on my behalf, and me second, that he'd be over himself on the first flight he could get, with a straitjacket in one hand, and a shillelagh in the other.

When the matron opened the door of the room and ushered Jack in, I jumped up and threw my-self into his arms without giving him a chance to say a word. Waiting for him to arrive, I have to admit I was more than a little scared. I had no idea how he felt about my never letting him know where I was, or what I was doing. Of course, I hoped he would understand a girl couldn't just write the man she really and truly loved and tell him she was making her living as a whore. Some things just aren't done, no matter how much of a free-thinker a person might be. I certainly could never be accused of being much of a conservative about anything. I'd broken every rule in the book without a second thought, because heritage and culture were two things I just didn't give a shit about. But even I didn't have the guts to write Jack about what I was doing. How could I explain it? Actually, of course, I didn't write him for another reason as well. I didn't want to let him know where I was, because the first thing he'd do would be to come after me. I figured if he wanted to take me back home, let him find me. There were lots of times in my life when Jack showed he could be a very determined man. And I decided this was one time he'd have to make his own decision. A girl, even a pretty one, can chase a man just so long before she gets to be a royal pain in the ass.

After kissing me and looking me over to make sure I was all in one piece, he sat down on the bench, with me next to him and holding onto his hand as tightly as I could. Gosh! He was still the handsomest man I'd ever seen, though he did look tired and a little beat-up. I knew why too. Chasing girls all over town every night can get to be hard work, especially if the guy doing the chasing feels he has to score with everyone he catches. But just being near him made my heart begin to jump and my breath become a little short, the same as always. Also, it started that old familiar itch down in my pussy. And now that he knew I'd been using that part of me, doing the very thing it was meant for, maybe he'd get the urge to see what it was like himself. If he only would, I wouldn't care what

146

he did to me for running off. If it made him feel any better, he could turn me over and wallop me every day for the rest of my life. Here in England, I'd been paid damn good money for letting men wallop me, and I'd stood up under some solid firing too. Not that it would make his feel any better, because no matter how many times my ass was on the receiving end, the next one stung just as much. But Jack was different from other guys. He could do it for nothing, all he wanted, if only I could be sure he really cared for me. And who knows? Maybe he might develop a few of the same notions these crazy English characters did. After all, if I remember correctly, he told me once his family had originally come from here.

"Well, Brick?" he grunted, trying to look very stern, but unable to hide the little crinkles of humor in the corners of his eyes.

"Jack! I . . . oh, I'm so glad you came!"

"Why? Because your cute little ass is in a jam?"

"That's not fair!" I protested. "And do you really think it's cute?"

"Yes. But why isn't it fair?"

"Because you're the reason I'm in a jam," I muttered, managing to squeeze a couple of tears from each eye.

"Me?"

"Yes, you!"

"What did I do?"

"N-nothing. That's the trouble!"

"Maybe you better tell me all about it. But first, how about turning off those crocodile tears."

"Crocodile tears?"

"Yeah. That was a cute trick when you were a little girl. But after what you've been doing, don't you think you're past the age for that baloney?"

"You mean . . . you knew I was faking . . . all the times I . . . ?"

"Certainly! But I figured if you thought you were fooling me, I'd go along with the gag."

That's when I really started to bawl, sobbing and wailing and gulping like a little kid. Imagine! All those times I thought I was taking him for a ride, he was really taking me. What a crock! But at the same time, it made me so happy, I didn't know what else to do but spill over. And when a female's feeling happiest, that's when she cries the hardest. I know it's ass-backwards, but that's the way us girls are put together. Jack, though, seemed to be quite used to it. He just took the handkerchief out of his breast pocket and handed it to me.

"Here!" he muttered, a little embarrassed by all the water pouring from my eyes. "Blow your nose and quiet down. I want to know why your running away to become a fancy whore is all my fault."

"You never looked at me!"

"That's a damn lie!" he insisted. "I looked at you every day . . . two or three times!"

"Sure! But you never saw me as a person. To you I was only that little brat you were saddled with!"

"I was never saddled with you," he murmured, pulling me into his arms and holding me close. "I took you because I wanted you. You were such a cute little girl and I was crazy about you. I still am."

"Why didn't you ever tell me?"

"I did tell you," he muttered. "In the only way I knew. By dressing you as well as I could, and sending you to the best schools I could find. Even sending you to that nutty psychiatrist when you

148

came back from the Bar-Nothing. What I should have done was spank the daylights out of you!"

"If you only had!"

"Why?"

"Over here, in the whore racket, a girl gets her ass smacked by every customer. It's the only way these limey lords can work themselves into the mood. They're the most mixed-up bastards you ever saw. You told me once your family came from England too. So don't you see? If you had, maybe . . ."

"It would never have worked. My family wasn't nobility. They were plain, honest, hard-working yeomen."

"Anyway, I thought you were getting tired of me," I sobbed. "You used to go out, night after night, chasing after those silly glamour girls. I thought you'd be glad to get rid of me."

"Never!"

"And I've been in love with you for so long."

"With me?"

"Yes, you dope! As a woman, not as . . . as a daughter. That's why I always got into so much trouble. You wouldn't pay any attention to me. And I figured if I couldn't have you, I'd do it with anyone who came along."

"When did all this start?"

"When I was nine when I went to camp the first time. That's where I learned to pussy-pet. And I found out if I kept thinking of you while I did it, it was better. I used to dream you were fucking me."

"Oh, no!"

"Oh, yes! I still dream of you. Only now, I don't pussy-pet anymore. I fuck instead."

149

"Is that why you started in with that Indian boy out at the ranch?"

"Why else? I have racial pride too. That redskin never meant anything to me. But he was there, he was willing, and it seemed like a good chance to find out what fucking was really like."

"Was it as good as you thought it would be?"

"Oh, it was wonderful," I sighed. "But it wasn't enough. I wanted the man inside me to be you."

"What am I going to do about you?" asked Jack softly, shaking his head. "The authorities here want to send you to one of their reform schools to try and straighten you out."

"Can they?"

"I'm afraid so," he nodded. "But I told them I thought it would be better if I took you home. They half agreed."

"There's something I have to know first."

"What?"

"If I do come home, how are you going to treat me?"

"I don't understand."

"Are you going to keep on running after all your girls and just pat me on the head every time you leave the house?"

"You wouldn't like that, huh?"

"No."

"O.K. What would you like?"

"This!" I said. And reaching up, I put my arms around his neck and kissed him the way I'd learned.

"Wow!" he muttered after a moment, taking a deep breath. "Wow!"

"That's what I want," I whispered in his ear. "And I'm a hell of a lot better at it than those others. I'm a pro!"

"Hmmm!"

"I want to sleep in your bed, I want to hold you in my arms, and I want to fuck you like crazy. I even want to kiss the king whenever I feel like it."

"What do you mean . . . kiss the king?"

"It's a game I learned from a Scotsman."

"What's it like?"

"I'll tell you all about it," I murmured, getting on his lap and feeling his pecker start to swell as I wriggled around. "But after we're married."

"Married! Don't you think you're a little young?"

I hugged him as tightly as I could, rubbing my bottom back and forth across his swollen pecker at the same time, and mashing my tits up against his chest. Then I kissed him again, even more thoroughly than the last time. "Do you?" I asked.

"No, by God! I don't!"

"There's just one more thing."

"What?" he asked hoarsely, holding me so tightly I could hardly breathe.

"Olga."

"Who the hell's Olga?"

"My Amazon mamma!"

"What's that?"

"A big, good-natured Swedish broad who worked for Mrs. Adams in her whorehouse. She watched over me when I was getting started. And she's wonderful! She's probably the best masseuse in the whole world. Just wait till she works on you."

"Where is she?"

"In the can . . . I think."

"And what do you want to do about her?" he asked.

"Take her with us, of course," I whispered, sighing with contentment as I snuggled in his arms, dreaming wildly about my wedding night.

151

There were more stars in the sky than I had ever seen before. And none of them looked anything like pearls either. To my eyes, they looked a lot more like diamonds, the kind of rocks that can only be found in collections like the Crown Jewels, which the English have got locked up in the Tower of London. But I suppose the sky always seems special to a new bride. There's something about a girl's wedding night that makes it different from every other night in her life. Just why I can't say. It certainly can't be the fucking, or the fact that for the first time in her life she can relax in bed with a man without having to worry about anyone finding out. In the first place, everybody knows what she's doing. In the second place, and this goes for her single girl friends, they're jealous. And in the third place, in this day and age, very few girls arrive at the altar in pristine condition in the first place, having been fucking for one boy or another, usually, since they were twelve or thirteen. I was one who always called that goupy kind of stuff a crock of shit. Oh, I wanted to get married as much as the next girl. If I hadn't, for Christ's sake, why would I have gone to all the trouble I did, when I could have stayed home, sitting on my ass and taking it easy. But now that it had happened to me too, I was beginning to understand why every bride is always beautiful on her wedding day. She may look exactly like a mud fence for the rest of her life. But when she takes that walk down the aisle, she's radiant. Why not? She's got it made!

Of course, I couldn't see too much of the sky. A porthole aboard ship isn't the best place in the world to look at the sky from. But even so, what I could see made little shivers run all the way down my back, ending up right in the middle of what fancy-pants literary books would call my "loins." I preferred to be much more down to earth and say I had a pussyful of goose bumps. I looked hopefully over toward the bunk where my lord and master was sleeping away. I wanted him to come over and stare out of this goddamn porthole with me, but the poor guy was dead to the world. And from the way he was snoring, I wasn't too sure whether he'd even want to get up in the morning. In spite of everything you hear, I guess women are just more sentimental than men. Because the night, and the stars, and his getting married, meant no more to Jack at this moment than a stale ham sandwich. After a while, I suppose, he'd begin to notice that he had a steady bed partner to snuggle up to his back during the nights, wake him up in the mornings by kissing him where no man ought to be kissed who has to get right up out of bed and go to work, and to compete with him constantly for first dibs on the bathroom. But I know you won't be able to understand what I'm talking about till I fill you in on what led up to this night, in this crummy little cabin, aboard this crummy ship, with my husband snoring away in his bunk while I wandered around in the darkness, in the sexiest goddamn nightgown anyone ever saw, dying for him to wake up and perform his marital functions. Now isn't that one hell of a way to describe fucking?

When Jack, with the aid and advice of the American embassy in London, told the authorities he wanted to marry me and take me off their hands, I think they breathed a large sigh of relief, in a reserved English way, of course. It would have

153

been an easy thing for them simply to lock me away in some reform school for girls, where the matrons would probably try to beat a little decorum into my head by way of my ass end. After all, I was only sixteen, and to them still a child. But they faced another problem that was beyond their doing much about. And that was that several important foreign government officials had been involved with me in a rather intimate way, and they were willing to agree to anything that would get me out of the country with my mouth shut. News reporters, from all over the world, were dying to find out the details of the story. And if I decided to spill the beans, there were going to be a lot of red faces in a lot of highly sensitive places. Governments might even fall. Even the Queen was anxious for me to leave, because of the visits certain members of the Royal Family had made to Mrs. Adams'. So once they were sure Jack really meant what he said, they were delighted. So much so, as a matter of fact, they were more than happy to toss Olga in as part of the deal. That poor woman was so happy to see me, and get out of the pokey herself, she broke down and cried like a baby. It must have made a pretty ridiculous picture. Our reunion, I mean. I was all of about one-quarter her size. And yet there I was, in a hotel room in London, trying to take the big ox on my lap and comfort her. Jack howled with laughter. And thank God, they took to each other on sight. The first thing she did, after she stopped crying, was to grab him, strip him down to the skin, and give him a rubdown that left him feeling so wonderful, he actually kissed her. And believe me, anyone who took a good look at Olga would have to agree, that goodhearted or not, she didn't exactly have the kind of face a person would want to kiss.

Anyway, the authorities gave us twenty-four hours to get lost. Naturally, I wanted to sail for home in style, on something like the Queen Mary, or some other ship of that kind. But the only thing leaving when we had to was a lousy freighter. And that's what we had to take. I suppose we were lucky at that to find it was headed for New York. We could have found ourselves on a tub going to Madagascar. I didn't even have time to buy anything for my trousseau. It was lucky I had this sexy nightgown. Originally, I'd bought it for a different reason, but it would do for a wedding night, which was why I was wearing it. We had a quick trip to the docks in a car ordered for us by the embassy, and the three of us were bundled up the gangplank and onto that ship without so much as a chance to wave good-bye to three or four spectators, old salts, who happened to be watching with envy in their eyes. And once aboard, we had to stay below decks until we were out of the river. The government was taking no chances. They were delighted to see us leave, and they weren't about to risk one of us getting left behind by mistake.

Jack had made arrangements with the captain of the freighter to perform the marriage ceremony for us once we'd reached the Channel, and it could be said we were on the high seas. I suppose it would have been nice to wait till we got to New York and have one of those big church affairs, with bridesmaids and everything. But I wasn't anxious to take a chance on his changing his mind. And anyway, who ever heard of a whore, reformed or not, in a white wedding dress with a

155

bridal veil? We sailed at nine o'clock in the evening, and the wedding was tentatively set for about twelve, which would make me a midnight bride. I liked that because it was almost like an elopement. As soon as we'd cleared the estuary, the water started to get a little rough. And as time went on, instead of getting better, it got worse. I began to notice, a tiny bit at a time, that Jack was becoming quieter and quieter. At first, it never occurred to me that a popular man-about-town, playboy, or whatever else you might want to call him, could possibly get seasick. But that's exactly what happened. And even though Olga and I stuffed him with all kinds of pills, by the time we were all up on the bridge for the ceremony, he was starting to turn a lovely shade of green.

As we stood in front of Captain Hansen, with Olga and the steward as witnesses, waiting impatiently for the clumsy squarehead to find the right place in the book, I suddenly reached out and took Jack's hand. I figured it was perfectly proper for a bride to hang on to her groom, not only for physical support but for moral as well. After all, a girl doesn't get married every day. But instead of my taking comfort from his hand, he clutched at mine like a drowning man going down for the third time. And by the time Captain Hansen had mumbled some of the words, and finally reached the place where he was supposed to ask each of us whether we'd love, honor, and obey, I had serious doubts about Jack's being able to answer. But he managed. When he asked me, I said "Yes" as quickly as I could. Then came the words all brides wait to hear: "I now pronounce you man and wife!" Very normally and a little excited, I closed my eyes and turned to my husband for the bridal kiss. I even opened my arms wide to enfold him. But after about ten seconds of standing there with my arms stuck out like a scarecrow, I opened my eyes to tell him a thing or two, but he wasn't anywhere in sight. All I could see was Captain Hansen, howling with laughter and slapping his leg like a lunatic. Even Olga was gone. Seeing my surprise, the captain motioned toward the railing enclosing the bridge deck outside. And there was my brand-new husband, with my Amazon hanging on to him, vomiting his guts out over the side. I rushed out to him.

"Jack!" I shouted. "Oh, Jack!"

"Leave me alone," he mumbled, turning his head so I wouldn't see the streaks of vomit on his chin. "I want to die!"

"Enough talk," Olga said abruptly. "We take to cabin now."

With Olga on one side and me on the other, we managed to get Jack down from the bridge and into our cabin. It's a good thing she was there too. I'd never have been able to handle the helpless reeling man by myself. Once there, we sat him down on the side of the bunk and started to peel off his messed-up clothing. It seems, in his dash for the rail, he didn't quite make it, and his jacket, shirt, and pants were drenched. But with his clothes almost off, it hit him again. Groaning, moaning, and spewing, all at the same time, he gave Olga and me the full treatment, all over both of us. I let out a yell like a Comanche on the warpath, but I guess Olga was more able to handle things like that. Without saying a word, she lifted Jack to her shoulder, his legs in back and his head hanging over in front, and rushed him over to the porthole. Motioning to me to unfasten it, she pushed his head right through the opening and let him go full blast, until there wasn't enough stuff left in him to fill a dwarf's thimble halfway to the top. Then, carrying him back to the bunk, she stripped off the rest of his clothes and shoved him under the blankets. From all the pills we'd fed him, and his exhaustion from vomiting, I think the poor guy was asleep before his head even touched the pillow. Having done what she could for Jack, Olga turned to me. Stripping me to the skin, she sprayed me with perfume, squirting it every place. Then she dropped my fancy nightgown over my head. Looking toward the bunk for a moment, she shook her head slowly. But when she turned back to me, she was grinning broadly, and slapped me hard on the behind.

"He wake soon," she chuckled. "Be much better. You see!"

"Gosh!" I sighed. "I hope so."

"Have good time! Good sleep! See in morning!"

Opening the cabin door, she left, closing it behind her with a slam and another loud chuckle. So there I was, wandering all around the cabin and staring out of the porthole, while my eager groom slept soundly in his bunk, completely unaware that I was with him or that he'd gotten married. Who would have believed I'd be legally wedded to one of the most notorious cocksmen in New York, and completely neglected on my wedding night? Nothing I'd ever heard of or read prepared me for a situation like this. For a minute or two, I wondered whether there might be a lonely sailor aboard I could call on for some pinch-hit duty. Because I was in the mood, and a bride has a right to expect a good fucking on her

158

wedding night. But finally, I decided that wasn't too good an idea.

At last, after a final look out of that goddamn porthole at the sky and the tossing water, reflecting starlight like glittering diamonds, I sighed, yanked that fancy gown up over my head, and crawled into my own bunk. The thing was never meant for sleeping anyway, only for luring. Besides, though I might be married to one of the most eligible guys around, and after all I'd gone through the last few months learning everything there was to learn about fucking, it began to look like I was going to spend my wedding night doing what I thought I'd never do again in my whole life. I was going to have to pussy-pet like crazy before I'd be able to get to sleep, and I didn't want those goddamn lacy skirts to get in my way.

———